MEDIUMS

MEDIUMS

Randy Ryan

MEDIUMS

Published by Pokeberry Press, a division of Pokeberry Exchange, LLC.,
New Castle, Pennsylvania

www.pokeberrypress.com

ISBN 978-1-951847-01-2

Printed in the United States of America.

Book Design by Stephen V. Ramey

I t is where all points converge—life, reality, heaven, hell, imagination—that holds the answer, a governing instability, a kind of hideous, unquantifiable creation-destruction. Don't try to comprehend. You can't. You're happier than you suspect without the burden of knowing the unknowable. Just settle on this for now. Whatever you sense, regardless of your condition, is all there is.

But if you come here, when you come here, new eyes will open. In a blinding flash, you will see there is an off switch for the universe, the heavens, the underworld, and everything conjoined and augmented beyond the invention of numbers. The Throne of Ultimate Chaos anchors it, creating hells out of heavens and hells out of hells.

And the Throne rests uneasy. That which breathes life into existence grows stressed, trembles with each titanic function. This, my tender ear, is the truth you dare not understand.

Book One

Terminal

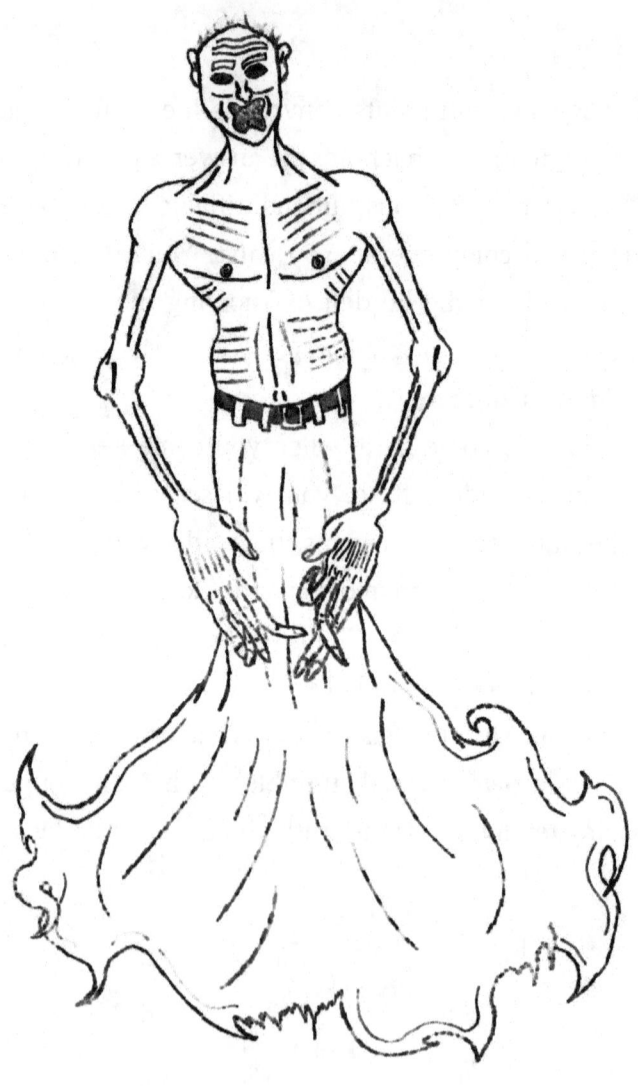

1

The news of the crimes was beginning to spread. In fact, the news had been spreading nationwide for the better part of two months. Mattie Ripper sat there and anxiously awaited the sound of the door opening, followed by the nurse's voice informing him that it was time for his appointment with Dr. Thorn. His passive eyes halfheartedly fixated on the television screen and the blazing fire reflected on its surface. A week had passed. It was November 7th and of the foliage beyond the window was still full and bright, but everything seemed more stark, drab and grey.

Mattie rubbed his eyes. Western Pennsylvania was nearing the middle ground between fall and winter. In the coming weeks, along with the arrival of Thanksgiving, the trees would become barren, high noon dull and overcast, the evening enveloped in stygian blackness before dinner. Just the night before, the world had fallen back, clocks set exactly one hour earlier. Normally, this was Mattie's favorite time of year, being that it was cold with shortened days. Turning the clocks back, however, meant an extra hour of sleep, and that meant Mattie had to suffer an additional 60 minutes of anticipation until he met with Doctor Thorn.

Look at all that chaos and destruction Mattie thought. He watched the burning remnants of the farmhouse on TV. The massive blue Dutch-colonial being consumed in what appeared to be eternal hellfire was located in a township Mattie had visited many times. Willoughby was part of the borough of Willow Falls, Mattie's hometown. He snapped out of his trancelike state. That chaotic, burning upheaval mirrored his internal state-of-being. The mass murderer, who'd claimed the lives of nearly twenty people since the beginning of September, had gone to school with him up until the third grade.

The door opened with an unnerving creak. The nurse, a dark-skinned, dark-haired woman of medium height and a name tag which read Mimi, stood in the doorway. She wore a white medical coat over her scrubs and dutifully read through the paperwork attached to her proverbial clipboard.

"Matthew Ripper," she called out.

Mattie was both relieved and sickened. He no longer had to watch that hellish fire, but this was no ordinary office visit. His heavy legs carried him out of the decidedly sterile waiting room in which the only colors came from a collection of magazines in a wicker basket (and the news on the screen).

He followed the nurse. The hallway was long and narrow, and equally bland. Every scent tasted like cotton swabs, penicillin, tongue depressors and cold, reflective steel. He felt as if he were being led to the gallows. *Urgent,* the receptionist's voice mail had stated. This could not be good.

They came to a room on near the end of the hall. Mimi left him with hardly a word, other than hollowly assuring him that the doctor would be right in. Mattie sat on a blue cushion at the end of a recliner-like seat, up high on cold metal, itself very susceptible to dents. Paper crumpled beneath the cushion. His feet touched the floor. The room wasn't two-by-four, but it was damn near close.

He examined a poster on the wall depicting human anatomy, every bone, muscle, artery, organ, tendon and ligament labeled in small, impossible-to-read print. His eyes lingered on the small intestine. That was where he had first experienced the pinching sensation, the throbbing discomfort that kept him awake. *Cancer?* he thought, putting words to the unspoken dread of past days and weeks.

The door clicked, the J-shaped knob turned, and Dr. Thorn walked in. He was a tall, broad man, roughly six-foot-two, with a bulky, boxy, almost square physique. Salt-and-pepper hair contrasted his mildly tan skin.

Thorn cleared his throat. He licked the tip of his finger and flipped through the two or three pages attached to the clipboard. When he faced Mattie his normally stern demeanor softened. He seemed pensive. No, pensive wasn't the right word. Apprehensive? Mattie couldn't quite put his finger on it.

"What's the prognosis?" he blurted. He wanted this dreadful, ungodly, indescribable feeling turning his stomach inside out to go away.

"Not good," Thorn answered bluntly.

"What do you mean by that? What did the tests show?" Please, God, tell me I didn't go through all that discomfort for nothing. MRI's, CAT scans, dye injection, palpitations.

Dr. Thorn's response was quick, precise, overbearing: "Terminal."

Mattie gulped. "How…how long do I have?"

"I'm afraid it's only a matter of weeks," Thorn said. "Maybe a month or two. You have advance acute Leukemia, which is far deadlier than chronic, especially in adults. I can refer you to a specialist. If you'd like a second opinion, that is. To be blunt, I'm not confident it would make a difference, but that's *my* opinion."

An elephant bigger than any in existence squatted on Mattie's chest. His vocal cords cramped.

"We've caught it too late," Thorn said with a half-hearted shrug. "Unfortunately, the key to cancer is catching it. Stage four is one monster, but yours has spread to just about every major organ—brain, lungs, kidneys—you name it. The metastasis is rather severe. There's really not much left to be done. If you'd like, if it would help, there's a great hospice I can refer you to."

Mattie sensed that Thorn was stating his due diligence, no compassion, no concern. What was there to be concerned about? Especially when you already knew the outcome?

"I can see that you need some time to think this over," Thorn said. "Let it settle in. My advice is to make as many arrangements as possible, spend as much time with your loved ones as you can."

Thorn glanced at his watch. "The nurse at the desk will give you a card with my contact information." Without another sound, his coattails vanished through the doorway, trailed by the closing slam of the door, the final exclamation point of Mattie's life.

When, at last, he found the strength to make his exit, the room was not entirely vacant. Neither Mattie nor his doctor had sensed the presence that had been in there with them all along.

It was not human.

2

The ride home was almost impossible. If Mattie had anybody who cared enough to come with him, they could've driven. But it seemed like that was too much to ask even of his father who lived with Mattie and depended upon him for nearly everything. *Knock it off*, he thought. *You're not mad at your father.* His hand went to his stomach, which had started its usual dull throb.

The beauty of the outdoors was nothing but a cruel reminder. The foliage, a bright collage of autumnal colors pitted against the gloom of the overcast sky, seemed to taunt him. *This is the beauty that will be taken from you.* What a sick, twisted joke. Thanksgiving was fast approaching, and it was Mattie's favorite holiday. How was he going to endure this one, knowing it would be his last?

He pulled up to his house on Lathrop Street, which branched off of East Washington. With the exception of its pointed roof, the blue, two-story house was perfectly square.

Ripper barked from behind the wooden fence. Mattie tried to walk him as much as possible. He felt sympathy for the animal and also for his father. He was a caregiver to his father and now he was going to need one himself. Every Wednesday, two home nurses would stop in and do the things that Mattie was required to do the other six days of the week, but without the training.

Their house was on top of a little hill. The hill itself was lush green and vibrant during the summer. Now, one week after Halloween, the grass was short and brown. Mattie trudged up the mini-hill and the four stairs to the front porch. The front door was in his way. His father would be waiting on the other side. The hard part wasn't over.

He stepped inside the warmth and familiar sights of his house. His father was on the couch, staring at the grainy images on the old-fashioned floor model TV. He was watching an old horror VHS tape.

After Mr. Ripper's wife died unexpectedly of a heart attack, he found himself in a state of severe depression. Food and alcohol were his crutch. Addictive predispositions were inherent in that side of the family. He ballooned up to over 600 pounds. It was a disgusting sight.

"Where've you been, boy," Mr. Ripper wheezed without removing his eyes from the fuzzy screen. "Don't you know it's suppertime? Fix me something to eat, I'm dying over here."

Mattie wanted to embrace his father despite his secret repulsion. He wanted to cry into those endless rolls of fat. Instead, he walked to the kitchen and stared blankly into the refrigerator. Thankfully, there was some leftover hamburger from last night's dinner. He slapped the oversized patty on an equally comical dinner plate and threw it into the microwave for a minute. He cut a large Keizer roll in half, slapped on the burger, its greasy juices staining the bread, and topped it off with lettuce, real mayonnaise, a tomato, and a healthy dollop of black pepper.

Mattie set the tray on a folding table within his father's reach. Mr. Ripper ravenously tore into his meal. His lips smacked, his mouth was open as he chewed, and saliva drizzled down his multiple chins. Mattie quickly made for the staircase. "Let me know if you need anything else," he whispered in passing. His father began swishing mouthfuls of buttermilk around his ground–down food.

"Don't go too far," he spat through his stuffed face. "I know you don't have a girlfriend, so you're probably going to go and tug on your pecker, but don't make a day of it. I'm gonna be wanting something to satisfy my sweet tooth here pretty soon, but probably another burger before that."

Mattie burst into his room, closed the door behind him, and collapsed onto his bed. He caught a glimpse of himself in the mirror How much longer would that relatively healthy appearance last? Although he didn't pay much mind to his looks, he knew he was going to transform into somebody unrecognizable. His olive skin, close-cropped dark hair, his eyes that seemed to change color depending on which shirt he wore, were all going to deteriorate. He would become a stranger to himself. There was no easy way to process this. The only thing to do was to shut down completely.

That is when he heard the voice.

3

here do we go from here?

It came to him in the same random fashion that a lot of thoughts occur to people. This wasn't a thought. It was intrusive, unwelcome. Was the cancer speaking to him? Mattie was terrified beyond measure.

"Who is this? What's going on?"

Never mind the clichéd questions, the voice responded with a hint of irritation. *Again, I will repeat myself: Where do we go from here? This is the question you are asking yourself, the dilemmas which so strongly imposes itself in your opposition, is it not?*

It is, thought Mattie feebly. He could barely hear himself inside of his own head, but the voice did.

I'm not going to waste our valuable time, it assured him. *I know what's precious to you, I know what's precious to all, and I am here to tell you that there is a way I can help. In an instant, I can have all your current concerns resolved, but you must submit yourself to me. That is my one and only offer. Do you submit?*

"I don't even know who, what, you are."

Not your whole self. The part that you that is imperfect.

"My cancer," Mattie whispered. "That's what you're talking about, isn't it?"

Indeed, it is. So, give it to me. Give it all to me. Allow me to take it off your hands.

"Why?"

Because I want it. Because I can. It is in my nature.

"What is your name?"

Think of me as The Voice Man. If I were to tell you my name, you would be dead faster than any cancer can dispose of you. Clear your mind. Let nothing else in.

God, if you can help, Mattie prayed, *now would be a good time to intervene, even if saving me means letting me die.* Mattie rolled his legs over the edge of the bed and stood. He stared into the mirror.

This was not his reflection. The closer he looked, the more he realized the features were not exactly his. They were misshapen. The forces it emanated were negative and diseased.

This is what I can take. The disease and unhope that will destroy you. A look of recognition dawned on the mirror-face. It could hear The Voice Man too.

Nod once if you submit.

Mattie glared as the image in the mirror—and presumably he himself—nodded.

This is Gunner Bane, The Voice Man said. *It will serve me. If you attempt to stop it, or interfere with its plans to the slightest degree, your cancer will instantly be restored. You have no choice. Relish in your new beginning.*

With that, Mattie felt The Voice Man leave his head. A lightening of pressure, and Gunner Bane dissapeared with a vacuum pop, leaving Mattie gazing confusedly at his reflection.

"What have I done?" he whispered. Others were in danger, he sensed, although he didn't know who or how many, and that was terrifying. No deal with the devil came without conseqeuence.

He walked to the window. His legs were no longer heavy. There was no pinch in his gut. The glass was cold. Outside, wind wailed like tortured mental patients and leaves scattered upon it. It felt wrong.

"What have I unleashed?"

4

Stephen Greenling had always been creative. He liked to fancy himself an Imaginer. His obsession with art and literature stemmed back to his childhood. With Christmas fast approaching, he'd been flooded with colorful nostalgia as sweet and sentimental as childhood friends and homes.

It was the 15th of November. The days were continuously growing shorter, colder and darker. He stared through his office window and ruminated on his next novel. At twenty-nine, he had already completed five novels, a dissertation, and two screenplays.

In his teens, Stephen had written an entire children's fantasy series about a boy named Hunter, because he was always searching for something. He had even done the illustrations. He'd modeled his project on R.L Stine's *Goosebumps* series, with its wonderful cover art and creepy yet funny content.

The day waxed and waned rather quickly. While Stephen had no class on Wednesday, he did have office hours until seven.

Most of his days were long, and he always returned home with a well-deserved sense of accomplishment. Being a Teaching Assistant was a job you did because you loved or you didn't do it, making 1,000 dollars a credit hour, which amounted to 3,000 over the course of four months. Stephen was more passionate about writing than teaching, but his basic writing class paid his tuition and stipend.

He checked his cellphone. It was quarter to six. The minutes were dragging by.

His office was on the second floor of Debartolo Hall, the English Department. The first and third floors were the American Studies and Anthropology departments respectively. The latter had a real lower jawbone, not a replica, of a Gigantopithecus Blacki, complete with oversized mandibles and all.

By the time Stephen got on the road, that jarring transition between fiery twilight and pitch black had taken place. He couldn't help but feel that somewhere out there in the blackness, eyes watched him.

It was a silly notion, but Stephen couldn't shake it. Nor could he rid himself of the idea that the darkness all around him was one big eye, or a set of eyes, watching and following him, moving alongside him as he drove.

After thirty minutes, he made it home to his dark, quiet house, which he'd recently just started renting. He looked forward to the solace of what remained of his evening. He glanced over his shoulder as he walked inside, before closing and locking the door with an audible click.

5

The feeling of being stalked was still with Stephen on Friday, November 17th. As he sat in his cozy home, it was snowing outside. Because he didn't have a garage, he would normally have to scrape his car off in the morning. Thankfully, tomorrow was Saturday and he had nowhere to go.

He turned the heater on in the bathroom, followed by the hot water, allowing the room to grow steamy. He jumped into the shower for a good long cleanse to purge himself of the day's stress, stick and grime.

When he hopped out, he wiped the mirror with a towel and evaluated. His features were plain, but round and loveable. His dark hair was matted to his forehead, damp with shower water. When he opened the bathroom door, steam emptied into the hallway.

He heard car doors closing, followed by locking and beeping. His younger siblings, Ezzy and David, were coming over to help him get his decorations up before the holidays were in full swing.

He remembered opening his favorite childhood gift, a toy from the Beast Wars toy line, a deluxe Dinobot action figure. The black barbarian box art inspired Stephen to draw in addition to writing.

Ezzy walked in, followed by David. Their cheeks were rosy. Stephen felt the bitterness of the cold coming from outside.

"Hurry in. Hurry in," he said laughingly. "There's a nip in the air. Christmas is right around the corner." They shuffled past, took off their coats and shoes, and got settled quickly into the warmth of Stephen's house.

Ezzy, whose full name was Esmeralda, was four years younger than Stephen, David nine years younger. Ezzy had graduated from nursing school that past spring, and was currently working at UPMC Jameson. She was considering going back to school to earn her BA to become a school nurse. She and David both had sandy blonde hair and dark eyes, unlike Stephen. Stephen, who liked to consider himself tall, actually found himself looking up to his little brother who was longer and leaner than him.

"Whew," said Ezzy. "I didn't know it was going to snow tonight, or that the temperature was going to drop like this."

David smiled, rubbing his hands together. "I looked at the forecast and they weren't calling for snow. But you know how that goes."

Stephen offered food and drinks. David helped himself to a glass of chocolate milk. "It's a tad early for eggnog," he said.

"Never too early for eggnog," Stephen said.

David had graduated from Willow Falls High that past spring, and was currently looking for work.

They got out the boxes of decorations. The boxes were new and unopened, like a fresh assortment of fruit and meat, reminding Stephen of The Ghost of Christmas Present's throne. They unwrapped the fresh décor, and began organizing it.

A set of eyes watched this festive tradition unfold. Gunner Bane didn't have to draw any closer than it was, nor did it have to focus or concentrate. The supernatural rods and cones in its dark eyes sent the basking warm glow of Stephen's house instantly to its brain.

ᛈ

Mattie Ripper also saw these images. For Mattie, they were headache-inducing, acid-fueled hot flashes that brought him to his knees as he tried to bathe his father. But there was someone, indeed something, else viewing this through Bane's eyes. The Voice Man that had transformed his disease into Gunner Bane.

With spikerlike precision, Gunner moved steadily closer, the crunch of frostbitten twigs and leaves unheard. The spindly, shadowy creature melded perfectly with the dark.

Cancerous breath fogged the window pane a sickly green as the fiend pressed close to observe the Greenlings partake in these festivities. Their joy twisted its necrotic guts and rendered Mattie immobile.

6

Thanksgiving came quickly. Mattie wanted to feel thankful, but his newfound health came with a price tag.

He didn't prepare much of a meal: turkey slices with gravy, green beans and mashed potatoes. He watched his father eat, listened to the smacking of those flabby wet lips. He wanted to empathize, but the man was just too gross. A pressure bulged in his stomach. It reminded him of the cancer, but the cancer was gone. This was an evil influence, Gunner Bane channeling its negative energy through his core. Mattie shuddered.

"Hey boy," Mr. Ripper slurred. "How about round two?"

"Yeah, happy Thanksgiving to you too, Dad." Mattie got up, trying to choke down a mouthful of potatoes. *Only a matter of time*, a voice purred. It wasn't The Voice Man, but the spidery tone of Gunner Bane.

7

The Greenlings celebrated Thanksgiving twice that year. The first time was on Thanksgiving, the 23rd, with Grandma and Grandpa Willower. Grandpa Willower had inspired Stephen's love of movies, introducing him to "John Carpenter's Halloween" and the definition of a classic.

Second Thanksgiving took place on the following Sunday at Stephen's fathers house. The Greenlings arrived in fine fashion. They ate, drank, laughed, and were very merry in each other's company. Dinner was followed by dessert, which was followed by a game of touch football. The sun shone in that special way that it does on Sundays, coupled with the magical warmth of twilight and the holiday season.

Throughout the festivities, something sinister festered within Stephen. As the sun set, its flaming descent showed prominently through the stark trees. Bony branches seemed to irritate the purpling sky like talons clawing at an infected eyeball.

David noticed the change. "It's gonna be dark soon. Let's go in."

After the relatives left, taking with them the excitement and laughter of the evening, Stephen felt vulnerable to the inexplicable threat he sensed. He wanted to drive home and dive under the covers. He wanted dawn to arrive.

"Come up to my room," David said. "I've done some rearranging, you know, since I don't have a job and all." He was an avid collector and had moved into the attic.

Stephen followed his brother up the creaky steps. A tiny window on the landing looked out onto the backyard. The sky was a deepening gloomy grey. Gunmetal with streaks of yellow lined the horizon.

"As you can see," David said, mimicking a tour guide, "we have this." A fish-belly blue-white shelf on the landing held *South Park* figures and various Hulk and Spiderman collectibles.

"Making our way to my room, we have this whole new display." David's parallel shelves, three in total, were filled with McFarlane figures and even more Marvel Selects.

Stephen was struck with the detail of these recently-purchased figures. He fondly remembered the smell that came off similar figures from his collecting years. There was nothing like the rich, heavy smell of plastic fresh from the box.

Stephen examined David's "Twisted X-Mas" figures, including Santa, Mrs. Clause, Rudy Reindeer, Jack Frost, Frosty the Snowman, and a gang of elves.

The dread intensified.

He forced his attention to the artwork displayed in David's room. Their mother had painted the back wall charcoal grey with black skyscrapers to resemble the skyline of New York City. It provided a nice contrast for David's childhood collectibles: rows of DVD's, stacks of comic books, and a pile of *Hank the Cow Dog* books whose pages smelled like the attic on a late, midsummer afternoon.

David plopped onto the foot of his bed and turned on his gaming console. *Oh, that's right,* Stephen remembered. They had planned to play *Friday the 13th*.

"Take some weight off," David said, patting the bedspread beside him. He took a bottle from the carrier next to the console. It was a lemon-flavored Twisted Tea.

"That's not going to do it for me tonight," Stephen said. He went downstairs to grab a scotch-flavored beer aged in an old barrel.

David was holding the Twisted Tea when Stephen returned. The iconic "KI-KI-KI, MA-MA-MA" echoed over the sound system as the lumbering bulk of Jason meandered onto the screen.

"Did you bring one for me?" David said.

"You have your own," Stephen said.

David took another swig, trying to power through the Twisted Tea as if it were the most tedious task imaginable. "Oh" he said. "Take that!" He was playing as the part nine version of Jason and had gone into rage mode. He grabbed a camper trying to escape. Stephen chuckled as a counselor's head came flying off in a splatter of gore.

David handed the controller to Stephen.

"That was nothing," Stephen said. When he pushed the button to return to the home screen, the controller vibrated wildly like it did when you made a kill. The vibration traveled through his hands, wrists, arms and shoulders. An image came to him. A man in a costume, some sort of hybrid between a werewolf, a scarecrow and a robot.

One side the fiend was all werewolf—fangs, hair and flannel clothing, complete with a dirty gardener's glove and bloody hacksaw. The other was chrome, cybernetics and scarecrow, a hellish contrast.

Stephen jerked back. The controller tumbled to the floor.

"What's in that drink?" David asked.

Stephen snapped momentarily out of his trance, but was quickly absorbed by the power again. The figure now wore a blocky, blue-green and turquoise striped sweater, bony, organic gloves (claws) and a velociraptor mask.

These are the keys which unlock my gateway.. Stephen cringed. There was a boldness to the voice that scared him, as if it had invented fear and death and none of the rules applied to it. That voice did not belong to the figure in his head, but rather the source of the figure in his head.

Certain happenings portend my arrival in your world, said the voice. These events emanate from your town. In fact, Willow Falls is the literal epicenter for my workings.

Violently misanthropic images and dark energy ripped through his mind, leaving him drained.

"What are you?" Stephen asked. He was close to fainting. *What kind of monster can do this? Create images and beings in my head?*

If I were to tell you, if your ears were to take in my name, allowing your brain to process it, especially spoken from me, you would suffer the most torturously instantaneous death metaphysical reality can produce and be condemned to a fate worse than...

"*Death,*" Stephen finished.

No, the voice answered: *A fate worse than Hell.*

What did it mean by that? Stephen sensed this thing's awareness far transcended anything logical. He wished it would end. He wished it could be as simple as saying he had to go, like ending a telephone conversation.

As if in answer to his prayer, the voice said, *I am going to allay your torture for the moment. You've endured just enough. Expect me.*

David grabbed the controller. "Why do you keep running into that wall, man?"

8

The dailygloom turned bleaker, more-stark, with longer, colder evenings and shorter days with sharper contrasts Mattie's dark impression of the landscape was no doubt linked to the being he'd loosed upon the world.

It was Thursday, the 5th of December. To think that there were still a good couple of weeks for it to get dark even earlier was a frightening prospect.

Mattie was fixing his father lunch early that afternoon. After lunch, it was going to be another round of Mattie's favorite activity, bath time. Bath time didn't consist of a tub or water or soap. It didn't even consist of getting off the couch. All Mattie needed was a wet rag, lightly doused with foaming bubbles, and some sanitary wet-naps.

Bologna frying in the pan was an admittedly heavenly scent. He scooped a generous portion onto a piece of whole wheat bread and slathered it in mayo. The heavenly scent disappeared. He slapped a pickle and a slice of provolone cheese on top.

Mattie would be lying to himself if he didn't admit his mouth was watering. He'd have to sneak himself a sandwich later, one without so much mayo.

"Hurry the hell up," his father wheezed. "What, did you decide to run upstairs and knock one off cause you haven't found a girl who can do it for you? Christ, I might as well get comfy then. It might be Christmas before I eat."

Mattie was more surprised than anything that his father had managed that many words in a single gust. Mattie could hear the rattle building in his chest.

The kitchen door burst open.

Mattie dropped a second piece of bread. "Damn." He leaned down to pick it up and wiped it on his pant leg. The door banged and flapped. An icy gust blew past him. There was nobody there.

Mattie went to close the door and a wailing came from everywhere at once. He shuddered. It sounded like the collective agony of dozens of suicide victims.

A horrible presence intruded. The doorknob was colder than anything. He pulled his hand away. A blue shimmer emerged from the wood and spread to the walls till the whole room was coated in ice. He heard a *crack* and turned to see the frying pan fractured in two.

Dad. Mattie rushed into the living room. Frigid air packed his lungs. The entire room was dark and frozen. His father sprawled wide-eyed on the couch. White clouds wheezed from his mouth.

Gunner Bane stood before him, a tall figure, easily six-and-a-half feet, freakishly skinny as if cancer had eaten down to the bone. Lifeless spider eyes watched Mattie. The creature's misshapen skull was fringed with grey wispy fuzz, hardly hair at all. It wore a dark, flowing cape like Mattie had seen in comic books. Mattie's gorge rose. He felt like he would puke.

"Why are you so fearful of seeing me?" Gunner Bane asked in an old man's voice.

"W-what are you h-here for?" Mattie managed through chittering teeth.

"It's been a month," Bane rasped. "You didn't think that all I was going to do was make my presence felt. This isn't a beauty contest. The very first thing on my agenda is to set you free."

"What d-do you plan to d-do?" Mattie wrapped his arms around himself to fight off the chill.

Gunner Bane's eyes turned to Mr. Ripper. "Oh, you will soon learn there are outcomes far worse than death." Its painfully crooked spider fingers extended to Mr. Ripper's cheek. Where it touched, skin blackened. Tendrils spread across Mr. Ripper's skull and amorphous neck. A choked gasp sounded.

Blue-white fire emanated from Bane's cape. The blackness continued until only Mr. Ripper's panicked eyes showed. A racket sounded. Ice crackling. Crystal fog enveloped Mr. Ripper's head and seeped down his massive frame until he was cocooned. Mattie tried to move, but was frozen in place.

Gunner Bane's hand turned and lifted. Mattie's father levitated. A snap of those deformed fingers, and the cocoon dissolved. Mr. Ripper's form pixilated. With a rush of static the pixels disappeared.

Bane turned to Mattie. "Fear not. You've done your part. Now rest." It strode through the front door. Wood shattered in its wake.

Mattie collapsed.

9

riday, December 9th. Stephen wasn't typically on campus on Fridays. He had to make a trip over to the campus Barnes and Noble to pick up a cap and gown for commencement on the 17th. His mother was more excited than anybody, Stephen included, to see him walk. He couldn't count the times she told him that having a master's degree, he was going to earn an adornment of tassels and a nice scarf.

David decided to go along for the ride. He would wait inside while Stephen ran in. The two of them would stop and grab a bite on the way home.

On the ride over, they listened to Christmas music, flipping back and forth between stations. David wanted to hear *Christmas Cannon Rock* by the Trans-Siberian Orchestra, and Stephen wanted to hear *Feliz Navidad*. As they neared Youngstown, the only station that came in with perfect clarity was mix 98.9.

The sun was high at one in the afternoon. Long, fleeting shadows flashed through the windows. Wooded fields on either side of the highway reminded Stephen of fall. The barren trees were beginning to coat with snow.

Youngstown roads were unpaved until they got off the Fifth Avenue and Belmont exit across from CVS. They passed DeBartolo Hall, as well as the student parking lot across the street, made their way down to the next intersection, and found the campus bookstore standing tall along the right-hand corner.

Stephen parked around back and hurried in, wanting to make this as fast as possible. The campus B&N was much more campus bookstore than actual Barnes and Noble. There was a row of bestsellers, but that was as far as it went. The rest was textbooks, campus authors, sweaters and trinkets.

It was surprisingly calm and quiet inside. With the exception of one or two female undergrads holding cappuccinos and browsing through hoodies, and a couple eating lunch at the café, there wasn't much confusion. Stephen relished the calmness. He hadn't forgotten his encounter with The Voice Man. He hadn't forgotten the images, if that was all they were.

He made his way to the second floor. An entire section was cordoned off. A laminated sign read "Cap and Gowns" with a big, bold arrow directing him to the left. A short, curly-haired woman with glasses asked if he was there to pick up his cap and gown.

"Guilty," said Stephen.

She passed him a clipboard. "Find your name on this list."

Stephen flipped through the first page. "Here. Greenling, comma, Stephen."

"That's an interesting name."

"Yeah, it's English. It's also a carnivorous fish."

"Cool. Write down an email other than your student email."

"You got it." Stephen wrote down his Gmail address.

She took the clipboard back. "Congratulations. What's your major?"

"Creative writing. I'm coming back next fall for a second masters."

She directed him to a tiny window where two more women asked the same questions and gave him a sheet of instructions for the following Sunday. He thanked them and headed back to the stairs. As he exited them, a colorful cover caught his eye.

The book stood out from a cluster of others. The spine was mostly black, with a touch of red—YSU colors. It was entitled *Perspectives,* the "T" capitalized to resemble a crucifix. On the cover, a creepily-crazed face of scarred skin stared through a Christmas wreath. Wide, grey eyes bore into Stephen, reminding him of Alex from *A Clockwork Orange.* A bony hand protruded from the bottom. Unkempt silver claws extended from its fingertips.

The book didn't feel right in Stephen's hand. It felt heavier than it should. It had a negative energy about it, maybe because of that maddened stare on the cover. He read the teaser on the back cover. The book took place in Willow Falls.

He quickly put it back. The last thing he needed was a book about suspicious happenings in his hometown. His encounter with The Voice Man was more than enough. Once his hands were free of it, he felt instantly relieved. He walked briskly away, cap and gown clutched to his chest.

What was it The Voice Man had said? Something about strange instances in Willow Falls that would herald his coming.

The book was a part of it. And what about those haunted house murders he'd read about?

Stephen darted to his car, not glancing left or right. His peripheral vision had brought him nothing but grief. He tried the door. It was locked. David slouched in the passenger seat, buds wedged into his ear canals. Stephen rapped on the window. David looked up. The door latch clicked. Stephen threw himself into the seat. He was panting.

"What's wrong?" David pulled the buds from his ears. Christmas music bled into the air.

"Nothing," Stephen said. "Just the setup in there is weird. It's too much like a campus bookstore. I'm not used to it." *I'm becoming the Grinch,* he thought, *thinking up lies and thinking them quick.*

"Oh. Well, where do you wanna eat?"

"McDonalds," Stephen answered bluntly. "I'm in the mood for a McChicken, a small fry and a sweet tea with a side of honey mustard sauce."

David chuckled. "That's what I was thinking too. But can we stop at the one back in town? I don't want to eat in this shithole."

Stephen nodded. "I wasn't planning on it."

Even after the Barnes and Noble was out of sight, Stephen felt eyes on him. He thought of the eyes on that cover and shivered. The sensation persisted even as they reached the Willow Falls city limits.

10

The following Thursday, December 22nd, the Greenlings made their annual trip to Our Gang's lounge and Kraynaks. It was actually was a bi-yearly tradition, once for Christmas and once for Easter. This year they were also celebrating Stephen's graduation.

Of course, it was packed, since Thursdays were Our Gangs wing night. Stephen loved this area, especially this year with so much weirdness going on in Willow Falls. He had done many book signings in this area, namely at the Shenango Valley Mall's annual "Meet the Author's" event held every October by a lovely little independent bookstore, Leana's Books and More. For the past three years Stephen had sold books there.

He followed his parents through the labyrinth of patrons and bustling waitresses to a big, black leather booth in a back corner. Stephen had reserved it earlier, knowing the restaurant would be crowded. In fact, he reserved this booth so often the bartender referred to it as "Greenlings Booth."

"Nice job with the reservation, Stephen," his dad said as he slid into the booth. "We can always count on *you*." He cast an accusing glance at David.

Stephen slid into the booth opposite his parents. It was comfortable. The waitress approached. Before she had a chance to say anything, David spoke up.

"I'll take a bucket of heaven wings."

She smiled and scribbled the order on her notepad. "And what will the rest of you be having?"

"A bucket of Jill-Zees," said Stephen.

"Twenty-five hot strawberry," said their dad.

"And a basket of regular and garlic fries," Ezzy added.

"Can we have an order of fried veggies for an appetizer?" asked Mrs. Greenling. "And cokes to drink, coke for everybody, with a pitcher of water."

They made their way uptown after dinner. Although Stephen had his own car, he still rode along with his parents. They never asked him to pitch in for dinner or gas. It was like being a kid.

Going from downtown Sharon to the upper part was a treat, especially this time of year. They passed the beautiful library, the warmly-lit Daffins, and several towering gothic mansions.

A somewhat smaller, but innately creepy building came into view. *Must be a funeral home,* Stephen thought. *Why didn't I notice it before?* A gaunt figure stood on the front lawn, silhouetted against a warm golden glow slapped onto the stone architecture by a line of floodlights. A chill came over Stephen.

It was the same haunting sensation he'd encountered in Willow Falls. *Certain happenings portend my arrival in your world.*

They arrived at Kraynack's packed parking lot. Everything now appeared to be darker, colder, and Stephen was very fearful of stepping foot outside the car. He did though, shuddering as the cold wind touched his skin.

Once they were inside, Stephen felt safer. He peered past shelves of knick knacks and antiques, through the glass protecting him from the solid black night.

"I saw a good horror movie last night," said David.

"On *my* Netflix," said their dad.

Stephen nodded. "Yeah, what was it?" He couldn't stop thinking of The Voice Man. *Am I putting my family in danger?*

They made their way through the store. Stephen inhaled the sweet, musty aroma and tried not to focus on the undercurrent of sick breath stench that came to him too often lately.

As he traversed Santa's Christmas land, a bone-chilling draft wafted from a hallway. Neither his family nor the other visitors recording videos on their phones noticed. The displays took on a sinister aura.

Stephen saw everything in perfect detail, the winter wonderlands, the anthropomorphic Christmas characters. There were M&M's and candy canes, country cottages with red, white, pink, purple and green candles melting in their windows, ice ponds and skaters and carolers, trees of different sizes, shapes, and colors ranging from green to white to blue to silver to pink to black.

Let the fear flow through you. Let it darken your innards and turn your blood BLACK so that I may devour you.

"You're not real," Stephen muttered under his breath. He forced his attention to the nearest display.

There was Santa, Rudolph, Frosty, Heat Miser, Snow Miser. Mrs. Clause, Jack Frost, Eon the Terrible, Baby New Year and Winterbolt. There was Father Time, Big Ben, Sev, OM (One Million), 1023, and even Old Mag the banshee from *The Leprechaun's Christmas Gold*. There was Scrapper the reindeer, Mother Nature, Sam Spangles, The Little Drummer Boy and Nester, the long-eared Christmas donkey. The display ended just past the Winter Warlock and Burgermeister Meisterburger.

As Mrs. Greenling was gathering their traditional bag of candy, an announcement came over the loudspeakers. "Attention shoppers. Our store will be closing in ten minutes. Please make your final purchases."

Stephen blinked. The store went dark. The air seemed to freeze around him. It was suddenly difficult to breathe. People became unmoving silhouettes. Everything was silent. No more Christmas music. No more rustling. A weird, cold phosphorescence coated everything.

A shadow emerged from the darkness, its black eyes more prominent than all the other darkness. Its gaping dinosaur jaw unhinged, spewing a cloud of hellacious breath.

"What do you want with me?" Stephen stammered. "You've been following me for weeks."

Sickening laughter reverberated. "Very clever indeed. You may refer to me as Gunner Bane. I was created from awry cells and phenomenal drops in temperature by my master, whom you know as The Voice Man."

"Why are you here?" Stephen demanded.

"My creation is not separate from my master's coming. This event is linear rather than distinguishable, as you would tend towards thinking."

"Why me?"

Bane laughed. "You will be targeted by other forces. Powerful ones which can complicate matters should you align with them. I'm here to issue a warning. Should you defy my master, this is what will become of you and your family."

A freezing cold projected from Bane. All around it, figures encrusted with frost and shattered—*Pop, Pop, Pop*—until the floor was covered with blood-red dust.

Lights came on. Music resumed. The Greenlings stood alone in the empty store.

11

Mattie hadn't been functioning well since the loss of his father. He carried on as best he could. He feared the day the police might come knocking at his door. *Will they think I murdered him? Did I?* He was at least complicit in evoking The Voice Man.

On the 22nd, a Friday, Mattie found himself at Big Lots. He used to go there with his mother when she was alive.

He wasn't looking for anything specific. The truth was, he needed to get out, get away. Remove himself. He walked aimlessly, almost blindly. The aisle smelled of cinnamon and Halloween. For the first time in weeks, he didn't feel watched. Maybe the Voice Man couldn't follow here where the strongest memories of his mother and childhood lingered.

The next aisle featured wreaths and garlands presaging Christmas. Wrapping paper filled one section. Then plastic mistletoe, singing Santa's, owls with light-up eyes, and nutcrackers.

He lingered at the end of the aisle. He wanted to buy something. Anything to make this last longer. He saw the cashier making change for a woman with streaked grey hair. He checked his pockets. He had a dime and three pennies. *What am I doing here? I have to leave sometime.*

He walked past the register.

"Did you find everything you need, sir?"

No, but I tried. He pushed through the glass door into freezing cold. Gunner Bane stood just outside, bathed in the twilight glow of the setting sun. Mattie's stomach clenched.

"What do you want?"

"You." Bane raised a shaky finger. "I need you to come with me."

"I'm not going with you. Why would I go with you?"

"I'm afraid, as they say, you have no choice." It pointed to the nearest cashier. "Unless you'd like me to take them, *all of them,* in lieu of yourself."

"What do you want me to do?" Mattie asked. "I thought your master cured me. The stress of you is pushing me over the edge."

"I do what I can," said Bane. A perverse smile, as if a house centipede could smile.

"To hell with you," Mattie said. "I'm going back inside where I'm safe."

"You were never safe." Bane moved through the glass and metal door, leaving a hole in its shape.

12

The Friday after Christmas, Stephen and David decided to go to the comic shop in Sharon. They left at noon, arriving there at twenty-five after. Stephen suggested they eat lunch at Our Gang's after.

The comics shop was a small, single-story building and could have easily been mistaken for a boarded-up house. The sign above the door read, in faded letters: Bennies Comics & More. David was mainly interested in the collectible figurines. Stephen planned to browse comics.

The shop seemed even smaller on the inside. Stephen was immediately taken with the sweet, musty smell. There were comics everywhere along the walls and in overstuffed crates, almost too many to take in. Stephen didn't know where to begin.

David migrated to the collectibles. A short man with an unkempt mullet stood behind the counter, reading *Venom and Carnage* by Pat Mulligan. He wore a Metallica shirt. *Must be Benny*, Stephen thought.

A Pokemon card caught Stephen's eye. *I haven't seen a Gyarados card in ages.* He lifted the pack and looked at the price. *It's going to be ages before I see it again.* He put the package back. In the slot below, he glimpsed a familiar image from his childhood.

It was a Beast Wars file card, known in the Transformers community as a Bio and Tech Specs Card. He caressed the plastic seal. Dinobot had always been his favorite. The black, barbaric body, wrought with protruding bones, gave it a very organic feel. The inverted, temple-like face reminded Stephen of the pyramid-shaped building covered in reflective blue-green glass along the main strip entering Sharon. Its outstretched arm held a fiery sword of bone.

There was just something magical about the character artwork. It inspired him, reminded him of his passion for drawing. It spoke to him in ways no human could, without words or gestures or verbal cues. Color, shape, detail, shading—all of these relayed significance. He reached for the card.

You've been expecting us. Here we are, and without a moment to spare. A great war is coming. You've seen its beginnings. This is why we needed you.

Stephen pulled his hand back. *What's happening to me?*

We need you. Of course, you could stand with any of the other Mediums. Siding with one of us IS siding with all of us. But WE need you, Stephen. You will lead us in a battle against…

The thought stopped cold. *They're afraid,* Stephen thought. He focused on the card. *You're talking about The Voice Man.*

Yes, we refer to the power that you and Mattie Ripper know as The Voice Man.

Who's Mattie Ripper?

He's the human from which Gunner Bane was carved. You will know him soon.

Carved?

13.8 billion years ago, matter and anti-matter collided in A Big Bang that is the direct cause of the universe. Before that, there were two beings. One was The Great Creator. The other was…The Other.

The Voice Man? What does any of this have to do with me?

Only in the realm of the imagination can illogical power exist that won't be cosmically mismatched.

David approached, seemingly out of nowhere. "You ready to go? I'm Starving."

Stephen's imagined conversation dissolved. He'd let the stress get to him, was all. He turned his attention from the character card to his very real brother. "Did you see anything you liked?"

"No, not really. Nothing that I don't already have. The stuff I don't have isn't anything I'd want to get anyway." Stephen laughed. David would never hesitate to buy anything he wanted.

They took one last look on their way out. Our Gangs wasn't packed at all, and they ate in great peace. The more Stephen thought about his interaction with an imaginary character from his childhood, the better he felt about it. It was an instinctive counterbalance to the Voice Man vibe that had haunted him for weeks, his psyche fighting back to right the ship. He wasn't going crazy, but recovering from a close call.

13

I t was the last day of the year, New Year's Eve. Stephen's Christmas decorations were still up. He never took them down until after New Year's Day. It was, after all, part of the holidays.

The Greenlings plans for tonight were relatively uneventful. David and Ezzy were coming over. He'd ordered plenty of take-out, and the three of them planned on simply sitting there and conversing while watching "New Year's Rocking Eve" live from Times Square. Stephen might partake of a beer or two, maybe three, but it was no big deal. Just another family gathering to bring in the new year. This year was different, though. The strange happenings in Sharon and being watched everywhere he went made the night feel more significant.

Hours melted away, but his feeling of unease didn't. He spoke when it was his turn, drank when it was his turn, but he wasn't really there.

Suddenly, it was 11:57 and the five-minute countdown was already two minutes in. The ball descended, slowly yet quickly. The weird sensation Stephen had repressed all night bloomed. Powers positive and negative pulled him in opposite directions.

As he watched the ball descend, a revelation came to him. When it hit bottom, the year would change and so would he. He couldn't shake the feeling that he would be different in his own flesh once the year gave way. What would it be? Would he fall victim to Gunner Bane's will or would his encounter with the Medium in Sharon protect him?

Outside in the woods, Gunner Bane grinned. "Silly mortal. All hail Titanos. Death fears Titanos."

Book Two

Internally Infernal Torment

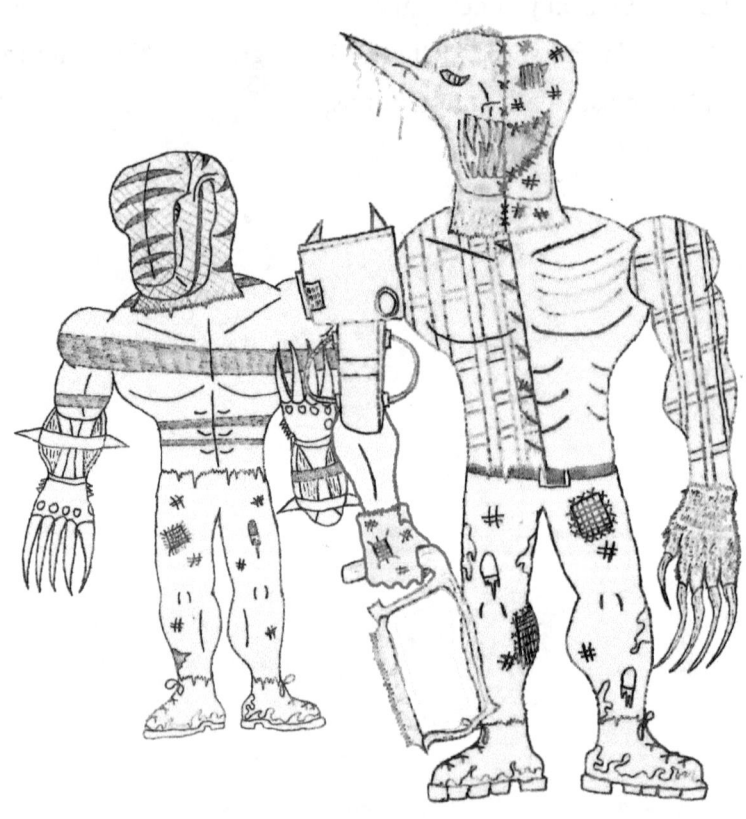

1

The new year had arrived in fine new year's fashion. It was bitterly cold and the residents of Willow Falls were well-aware it was only going to get worse. The *Farmer's Almanac* promised crushing loads of snow. Indeed, it was colder and snowier in Western Pennsylvania than it had been in many years.

Stephen felt Gunner Bane's sickly presence everywhere. Its vile breath rode on every biting gust. Snowflakes dancing outside the dining room window reminded Stephen of the disintegrating people in Kraynak's. He shuddered and turned from the window. Was that even real? How could it be? There'd been no sudden frenzy of reporting, no Facebook memes, just a smattering of missing persons reports. Even his parents had forgotten the event. If Stephen tried to broach the topic, they shut him down with small talk or some other breaking news story.

As he often did when life got crazy, Stephen turned to art. He went to his bedroom and rummaged through a pile of printouts by his copier. "Bingo," he said. Five sheets of pure white drawing paper. He opened his desk drawer and located a fine-point pencil and black pen.

Lines and shapes and details came easily. The pencil in his hand became a wand crafting magical images. In just under an hour, he had finished a portrait of sorts. Gunner Bane. All the hideous features were present, the sunken cheeks, sallow complexion, eyes so black they hurt. His jaw clenched. He wanted to rip the drawing to shreds, but it wouldn't do any good. It was complete, it was there. It now existed.

He positioned the next page. Maybe he could cancel the first drawing with something fruitful, positive, and productive. He didn't know what it would become, but and idea came quickly, then two, three, a hundred, seemingly all at once.

His chaotically creative confusion was short-lived. One concept emerged from the others. *Why don't I create a general?* A real, physical, tangible general. They had told him he would lead the army. That could work. Yes, sure it would. *I can make him, her, or it even more powerful than Bane.*

This general would be more than just a general. It would be the embodiment of all that he found appealing in *Beast Wars.* Ultimately, Stephen liked drawing things out of his head better than copying reality. Drawing from imagination was more satisfying than the arduous and eye-straining act of recreating mundane objects.

He drew and drew and drew until his creation gazed from wraparound segmented eyes on an insectoid face that reminded him of a praying mantis. *Clearly Dinobot inspired me.*

The body was ridiculous in its over-the-top, cartoonish musculature. Markings covered its exoskeleton. To the untrained eye, they looked like insignias on a skin-tight suit. In reality they were fanciful tattoos ranging from flame-like patterns, decorative bands, claw marks, a tiger, and even a scaly black serpent slithering through the holes of a die.

Stephen leaned back. His general was creative, inventive, artistic, as least to the degree his talents allowed. His gaze drifted to the creature's limbs. Its right hand was a fanciful sword, complete with a half-moon hilt. The left hand was more like a shield with a razor-sharp point.

"Yes," he said. This creature could defeat Gunner Bane.

2

A few days later, Mrs. Greenling and Ezzy decided to take a trip to the Beaver Valley Mall. Stephen, feeling better since his artistic rebirth, decided to go along. He'd always enjoyed the trip which consisted of long stretches of highway, toll booths, a couple bridges, valleys of hills and woods, a smog-shrouded industrial plant, and electrical towers perched on rocky outcroppings connected by high tension wires.

"I always feel like we're driving into one of the districts from *The Hunger Games* when we come through here," Ezzy said. Stephen gazed through the side window. Ezzy was right. The stark whiteness of the snow added to this dystopian effect.

Ezzy twisted in her seat, peering past the headrest. Stephen always let his sister ride up front. She tended to get carsick in the back.

"Do you have any good books I can read?"

"Do you have a specific genre in mind?" Stephen said,

"There's a lot I could recommend, but probably not a lot that you would like. "

"Have you read the Harry Potter books?" she asked.

"The first six."

"How are they? The movies are pretty good. Have you seen them?"

Stephen shook his head. "I like to wait until I finish the books."

"Your loss. Sometimes movies are better."

"That's your opinion."

She laughed and turned back to the front.

They turned left at the light on Beaver Valley Mall Road. Toys R'Us was on their right, and the main mall, a long, low brick building with many pocked signs lay ahead. The Books-A-Million (BAM!) sign stood out from the side of the building. Stephen's attention perked up. Maybe he would pick up that seventh Harry Potter book, *The Deathly Hallows.*

They parked near the main entrance and entered through the courtyard. Books-A-Million was to the right, FYE to the left. Stephen turned right.

"Where are you going?" Ezzy said.

"Books-A-Million, of course."

"Wait a minute. You're in a real rut. Come with me, I have something to show you."

"I told you I'm not into bath beads."

She laughed and grabbed his hand. "Come with me. You'll like it." She pulled him into FYE.

A bin of cheap DVD's blocked the main isle. Ezzy tugged him along. "Back here, back here. It's over here."

Steelbook editions of *Halloween 2* and *Halloween 3* faced outward from an eye-level shelf. Stephen was drawn to the cover of *Halloween 2* depicting Michael Myers engulfed in flames with blood tears running down his mask.

"See," Izzy said. "I told you. I'll leave you to it." She laughed and and walked away.

Stephen reached to feel the embossing on the cases. "Aren't you gorgeous." The cover image seemed to move, a series of still shots speeding up until it was almost real. Stephen's hand warmed. He pulled away.

A blur of firey images surrounded him until he felt as if he were in the burning hospital depicted on the cover. He heard the crackling flames, felt the heat drying his skin.

Voices swirled from the infermo. "We are cinema. We are the true power in your world. Embrace us, Stephen, before it's too late." Stephen's body tensed. The blood in his veins ran cold. He shivvered.

The scene fell away. He was back in the store.

3

Gunner Bane stirred within its encapsulation, a pocket in time and space that protected it from entropy and decay. It thought about Titanos and the font of all primal power. Green feelings of envy colored its mood. It didn't like to feel small.

The world beyond the capsules membrane appeared fractalized, a collection of crystals like the people it had touched and taken. Bane glanced over its bony shoulder. The Mattie-thing stood motionless. Bane scoffed. *Petty creature.* It was held together by nothing, not even will.

Bane gestured to bring its unwilling companion out of torpor, but there was too much power in that simple movement. Mattie's form began to drift apart. Bane felt a pulse of desire, a need to have it end. The Mattie thing wanted to die.

"No, I'm not done with you yet." Bane pulled the power back. Mattie's form solidified. It blinked viciouisly. It's mouth opened, exposing those bone-white teeth that fascinated Bane.

"Why are you doing this?" Mattie said. "Why did you heal me just to make me suffer?"

"I didn't heal you. I want you to see this." Bane touched the barrier. A portal opened. Willow Falls resolved into focus beneath them. The aerial viewpoint showed a map-like image, buildings covered in snow, roads and rivers cutting through the land like divisions between cells.

The view shifted and zoomed to Lathrope Street. Mattie's house took form its peaked roof covered in snow. A desperate jackhammer sound came from inside.

"Ripper," Mattie yelled. "What have you done to Ripper?"

Gunner laughed. "I've done nothing to your dog. You didn't let it out."

"How could I? You pulled me to this place against my will."

"Not my problem."

A lone figure stood on the sidewalk. "That's Mrs. Rupert," Mattie said. "She lives next door."

"Perfect." Gunner pointed its index finger.

"Stop," Mattie pleaded. "If you hurt—"

"One cell," Bane said. "That's all it takes. In one week, she'll be dead."

"Why?"

"Because I can. Because I want to."

4

After Stephen's encounter with cinema at FYE, he had binge-watched numerous series on Netflix, including *Masters of Horror* and *Game of Thrones*. In the past week he burned-out. If Cinema were influencing him, it was certainly being coy. Today he was writing.

Ezzy claimed movies were better. He remained unconvinced. Even total immersion in streaming video had not quenched his longing for more intimate worlds only accessible through the written word. He picked up his work in progress. As he read it, the voice of Literature emerged from his own internal voice. *We knew you'd join us, Stephen.*

After a momentary startle, he grinned and set the pages down. Of course he would join Literature. It was in his soul.

5

Stephen sat at his desk, penning furiously. He'd gotten out of bed before the alarm went off, still feeling last night's buzz. He had to be at YSU by eleven, but didn't want to stop. He could call in sick but that would set a bad precedent. He needed to push through this. He couldn't let himself get caught up in one passion, or one Medium. *Balance is key.*

He stopped and reread the last paragraph.

He understood that time was like a river. Branching and diverging into separate tangents. He only needed to figure out a way to fix them, influence them all.

Did I write that? It's good.

The inspiration for this book came from *Physics of The Impossible* by Michio Kaku and *Astrophysics for People in a Hurry* by Neil Degrasse Tyson. The action took place in an underwater world, a sort of Lovecraftian miasma of gelatinous substance infused with clusters of fine bubbles that fissioned into shapes and dissolved. It reminded Stephen of the marbled endpapers of his classic edition of *Frankenstein*. You could see through them but not quite.

In his mind's eye, bubbles gatheried in the outline of Frankenstein's monster. The shape morphed into Dracula, then Ebenezer Scrooge, Moby Dick, and Pitt from Image Comics. *It's was as if the bubbles moved in response to my imagination.* This was what the Mediums needed, a force to harness their passions, a hand to guide them in the right direction.

Could I be that force?

6

Over the next four days, Stephen became acutely aware of the influences of media on culture. And not only literature but art and film too. He'd been writing like never before, as if he were addicted to the process.

On Saturday afternoon he driove to Boardman to meet his college friends. The days were gradually getting longer, but there were still plenty of hints of cold, winter darkness. It had snowed overnight, but the roads were cleared. That was one thing about Western Pennsylvania and Eastern Ohio, they cleared their roads.

Everything he saw seemed to inspire him. Ice-laced trees became webs crawling with arachnids. An underpass led to a world of medieval magic.

He came to a beautiful sign. *Welcome to Poland Township, EST in 1796.* The old houses reminded him of history class and the revolutionary war.

His phone buzzed. *Don't' text while driving,* he thought. He laughed. This wasn't driving. Although Poland was very quaint and beautiful, the speed limit was 25 and if you found yourself going 26, especially with PA plates, chances were you'd get a speeding ticket.

It was a group text from Jen. *Hey guys I'm here a little early. Take your time, the roads are slick! I'll reserve our table. See yinz soon!* Stephen considered replying, then thought better of it.

He was about five minutes away. Traffic was stopped up on the bridge leading to Boardman, but beyond the light the country road opened into a six-lane highway with strip malls on either side. He felt as if he were on a precipice between worlds.

He passed a couple lights and turned into the parking lot. El Vallarta. He felt a tingle of excitement. It had been four months since they'd gotten together here before class to down a couple beers. Amy usually worked her way through a margarita while Jen ordered two or three or even four Sangrias. Brian was the designated driver type and preferred water with a lemon wedge.

He got out of his car and the cold hit him. The air wasn't particularly frigid but a strong westerly breeze maximized its effect. He pulled his jacket tighter. This reminded him of the people-statues at Kraynaks before they disintegrated. *Why doesn't that bother me? People died there. Am I some sort of monster?*

A car door slammed. "Hey, Stephen."

Stephen turned to find Brian unfolding out of his 1999 Chevette, dressed in his usual blue flannel shirt and beret tilted atop his shaggy blonde hair. His glasses winked in the dying sunlight.

"Hey, Brian. Jen reserved our table."

"Yeah, I was on the text."

"Sure." Stephen opened the restaurant door. A familiar smell of fried tortillas surrounded him. *Comfort food.*

Brian walked past. "I take it Amy is late."

Stephen laughed. "What's new about that?" He followed Brian in. The dim lighting and warmth were a welcome reprieve from the cold.

He spotted Jen at their table near the back. She was short. Her shoulders barely cleared the table's edge. Her big personality made up for it.

"Hey, guys. Stephen, did you read that book?"

"*Deathly Hallows*? Yeah, I finished it days ago. I'll be done with the whole series by March."

"Are you loving it?"

"She's not Lovecraft, but not bad."

He and Brian sat at the table. The waitress brought over menus. Jen ordered a sangria, Brian a water, this time with a lime.

"What's the occasion?" Stephen said. "I'll take a Yuengling."

The door burst open and in came Amy, red hair ablaze, thigh boots clomping. "Hey, did you see The Autopsy of Jane Doe?"

Heads turned. She was using her principal voice.

"As a matter of fact…" Brian's voice faded from Stephen's attention. An image flashed through his mind. In the movie, the coroner and his son had peeled back the skin of Jane Doe's torso to reveal tattoos on the inside of her flesh. His whole body went cold. The symbols were suddenly familiar.

Of course, they are, Gunner Bane wheezed. *I told you this is the only book you need.*

"Titanos," Stephen whispered. *What if this is inside me? Am I infecting my friends just by being here?*

He stood. "I have to go."

"What's wrong?" Jen said.

But Stephen was already pushing Amy aside and heading out the door.

7

The phone rang. Stephen stirred within his cocoon of blankets. He should've turned the ringer off, but the buzzing was somehow worse than the ringing.

It continued. "Moonlight Sonata" by Beethoven. At least it was bearable. It didn't stop. *Why isn't voicemail picking up?*

The ringtone repeated. "Oh, screw it."

He unwound himself from the covers. It felt like he hadn't left the bed for a week. Of course, he had. He had a disease, not a magic bladder.

"Yeah."

"How's it going bro? I've got great news. I asked Sharon to marry me and she said yes!" The voice was familiar.

"Jay?"

"Who else, bro?"

"Glad to hear it." Stephen tried to inject happiness into the words, but suspected he failed.

"We booked First Presbyterian on November 2nd, Jay said. "Mark your calendar."

I don't look that far ahead. None of us may be alive by then.

"I can't talk now, Jay."

"I want you to be my best man."

"Who in their right mind would want me?"

"Is everything all right? Are you sick?"

"You don't know the half of it." Stephen ended the call and turned the ringer off. Gooseflesh sprouted along his arms. He thought of the contagion spreading beneath his skin like tiny fingernails clawing to get out.

He'd almost reached the bed when the phone rang again. Didn't buzz, didn't vibrate, but rang, not "Moonlight Sonata" but another Beethoven piece. He couldn't remember the title.

He picked up. "I told you, Jay, this is not a good time."

"Silence," a distinguished voice said. "We prefer it to Moonlight Sonata."

The statement caught Stehen off guard. "Wasn't there a short story by Poe?"

"Precisely. 'Silence—A Fable'. 'Ours is a world of words.'"

Literature, Stephen thought.

"You cannot do this alone, Stephen. You should not hang up on your friends."

"Easy for you to say. You're not carrying this disease."

"Passion is a disease too, Stephen. It's up to us to determine which shall win."

8

Gunner Bane was well-aware of Stephen's association with the Mediums. *Mediums*. They were a militia standing against Titanos' omnipotence. Stephen would be crushed with them.

Bane knew it played a minor part in Titanos' plans, but an important one now. It's duty was to kick the hornet's nest and pave the way. With the Mattie-Thing out in the mortal world spreading disease, the way was indeed being paved.

Images bombarded its spiderlike eyes. Bubbles of perception. Simultaneously, it watched Amy, Jen, Brian and Jay going about their everyday lives. It was with Jen in her apartment behind Best Buy, panting at her every move. It was with Brian in his cozy house playing with his boy child. Couldn't he see how narcissistic that was? Amy had two miniatures, but at least they were older and less duplicatative. And Jay, blowing out candles on a cake. *How pathetic.* Titanos blew out suns, stars, entire constellations.

"I will gain such power if I play my part well," it said. Titanos had promised as much. Could it trust someone as boundless as Titanos? It dared not think too deeply about that.

It was also aware of Stephen's incessant scribbling. "How could so many useless words come from an inferior mind?" Bane hadn't taken Stephen's family off its hit list. For now, it was content to let them be. The more sympathizers Stephen sucked into this wheel of insanity, the more fun Bane would have.

9

Part of Stephen feared his involvement with the Mediums was delusional at best and insane at worst. The creature Gunner Bane would easily defeat his efforts. Chaos always defeated order. That was entropy.

He glanced at the *Guardians of the Galaxy* calendar on his wall. January was Groot, an unlikely hero. It was the 27th, nearing the end of the month. He needed to draw a new picture. He was thinking of a general with a chest full of metals. Something like he'd seen on a self-published book last week, only much better.

A challenge presented itself immediately. How could he hope to imbue this "general," this accumulation of lines on a page, with *real* power, the sort of power that could actually defeat a monster like Gunner Bane?

"I can try. I can do that much."

He stared at the blank page. Nothing called out. Still, he had to start somewhere. He made the first mark. *Cheek. Strong cheek bone.* "Yes, yes." *Now an eye. A bold, blue eye.*

The face was done. He started on the trap muscles. This was good. The general stared from the page as if he were real.

"He is, Stephen." All of a sudden and just like that, it happened. As soundlessly as light hitting an eye when a switch flips. He was still himself, but everything around him changed. He stood on an open plain, surrounded by lifelike figures of characters drawn from his youth. including the bony outline of Dinobot with his bio-mechanical jaws. Weapons covered him like the needles of a cactus.

Stephen's chest tightened. This was the character that had inspired him as a child. He remembered peeling the action figure from its plastic cocoon, how excited he had felt. *It's my imagination but what great detail.*

The crablike hand flexed. Stephen stepped back. His eyes fixed on the huge muscles of that arm. The vein he remembered so well from the character card popped out.

"You're real," Stephen gasped.

The creature's arm raised, lifting the spinal sword from its dinosaur form. The blade ignited. A great roar went up. Other figures came into view, a vast army of similar creatures.

You will lead us into battle, Art had told him at the comic shop.

Another figure stepped forward. Stephen recognized it immediately. This was the character he had drawn in homage to Dinobot. He was taller, thinner and more vibrant than the original, with the same insect face.

"Xyphactus," Stephen pronounced, naming his creation. He didn't know where the name came from, but it was perfect. He looked into its eyes and sensed contentment. It was grateful for the gift of life.

A cracking sounded. The ground began to shake. The sky blackened and a haze began to rain down. When it touched the creatures on the plain, steam hissed. The creatures melted, even Dinobot, until there was nothing more than puddles. But not *his* creation. Not Xyphactus.

A voice boomed from behind him "You think you've found comfort in this place?"

Stephen turned to find The Voice Man towering over him. Pressure swelled through his head. A disembodied chorus chanted. "All hail Titanos. Death fears Titanos."

"Normally, you would turn to stone if you heard my name. No mortal can withstand the primordial power of my being. I have shielded your puny senses this time. You will not be so fortunate should we meet again."

Titanos gripped the staff of its unique weapon. One end was an axe, the other a broad sword. The axe end radiated an intense heat that made Stephen sweat.

"Not all artistic representations will align with your purpose. Don't be misguided by your naïve faith in creation. Everything created is destroyed in the end." Titanos' eyes narrowed. "You see what remains of your army." Stephen sensed surprise.

Pounding footsteps approached. Wind buffeted Stephen as Xyphactus thundered past, webbed fingers flailing. The sword -arm slashed, striking Titanos' metal breastplate with a shower of sparks. The sword shattered into a billion pieces.

Titanos reeled back but recovered quickly. Its left hand

grasped Xyphactus' throat. Muscles corded on Xyphactus' back. Inch by inch, Titanos drove him to his knees.

"Fear me," Titanos said.

Tattoos peeled from Xyphactus' hide revealing an exoskeleton. Patches of skin flew at Titanos' face, covering its mouth, eyes and nostrils. With a growl, it tore the film of tattoos away and flung the mass aside.

Xyphactus stood. His arm had regenerated. The bony sword slashed Titanos' saurian face. Something like blood splattered.

Titanos swung its axe. Xyphactus shot backwards with such force the plain split around him. He was gone.

"All hail Titanos. Death fears Titanos."

Like a black hole, Titanos collapsed into itself. The pressure in Stephen's head alleviated.

10

Stephen sat at his desk, as he had done every day since his confrontation with the dark forces of his imagination. That's what this had to be. He was losing his mind. Some form of waking nightmare.

He stared at the partial illustration on his desk. It was supposed to be a heavily-armored version of Dinobot but looked more like a Ninja Turtle.

"This is useless," he said. He crumpled the paper and tossed it onto a knee-high pile of similarly crumpled pages by the bed.

He gazed through the window. February had arrived. The evening sky was streaked with powdery pink and scarlet. He thought of the blood spraying from his "army." *What a joke.*

The cellphone rang. *Eric Francis.* He almost didn't answer but he hadn't talked to Eric in ages.

"Yeah, what's up?"

"My man," Eric said. "Long time, no see."

"Yeah, I remember. Steel City last summer. You were drinking Miller Lite."

"What are you talking about? I'm a Dogfish IPA man."

There was a pause.

"I finished your book the other day," Eric said.

"Which one?"

"*The Macabre Mundane.*"

"Did you like it?"

"It's a thinker. I dig it. I one-hundred-percent couldn't envision it taking place anywhere else."

"That's the tone I was shooting for. Gotta be precise with your language, you know?"

"Absolutely."

"You think it would make a good movie?"

"Why don't you come over and talk about it? I got some spare Dogfish Heads waiting."

"I don't really feel up to it."

"Come on, it's been forever."

Stephen looked at the pile of crumpled paper. *Oh, what the hell.*

ᚦ

Two hours later, they sat by Eric's fireplace. Stephen was on his third Dogfish and the gloom was starting to lift.

Eric clinked his bottle to Stephen's. "Keep grinding, man. That's all you can do. I'll be there to support you every step of the way."

Stephen took a drink. The taste was mildly sour.

"Speaking of movies," Eric said, "Alyssa has a friend in California who's into that. Maybe she can hook you up."

"Where is Alyssa?" Alyssa was Eric's fiancée.

"Baking with her mom. She won't be back till late."

"Give her my love."

"You've got a real gift. I hope you use it for good."

Good. The word echoed in Stephen's mind. He was feeling relaxed, a little light-headed.

Maybe my gift isn't the visual arts, but the printed page.

He remembered the story he'd started months ago. *The Quantum Gate.* It was a story about cosmic power used in an epic battle of good vs evil. Just the thing he needed now.

11

The sickness was spreading. Bane widened the portal. Lathrop Street was busy today. *All the better to sow disease,* Bane thought. A grin split its spidery face. It saw the virus as glowing particles embedded in people, places and even their pets. Soon humans would be dropping in the middle of conversation. Bane would be one step closer to empowerment. Its whole body shivered. The outside world reacted. The sun flickered.

ᚦ

It was mid-March and Stephen had made great progress on his book. The strange happenings of February were starting to fade. He'd been writing and illustrating almost non-stop.

He looked through the window. It was a nice spring day. He should want to go outside but he didn't. For one thing, there was news of a nasty virus spreading through town, but mainly he didn't want to lose his momentum. He stretched and watched a squirrel raid the neighbor's bird feeder. It was amazing the contortions the little rodents went through just for a few kernels of seed. The light blinked. He looked up at the ceiling fixture. Another flicker. It wasn't the bulb, it was outside.

"What the…"

Help, a voice pleaded from the depths of his mind. A bubble expanded through his thoughts. He saw a map of Willow Falls. It was a beautifully-rendered map, as if a cartographer from the 1800's had made it. He squeezed his eyes closed and rubbed his forehead. This was all he needed, more strangeness. He started drawing again.

Something pushed him. He threw the pen down. Ink spattered across the page, staining his newest creation—a humanoid ceratopsian with heavily-armored weaponry and hide.

Another push. *HELP!* The map behind his eyes pulsed insistently. It was the Mediums. It had to be them.

"All right, I'm coming."

Apparently, February wasn't over.

ᚦ

The car started first try even though he hadn't driven in three weeks. He pulled away from the curb. He wasn't sure where he was supposed to go, but knew it was southeast. As he pulled up to the first stop sign, the GPS came on.

"Turn left in 500 feet." It wasn't the usual smarmy female, but a male voice with a metallic tinge.

The voice led him to a house on the east side. To all appearances, it was just another rowhouse. A blocky blue structure with a narrow plank fence between the neighbors. He didn't want to continue. This whole mess was a fool's errand.

Still, he suspected the Mediums wouldn't let him rest until he complied.

He shut off the engine, got out, navigated a cracked sidewalk, and climbed steps to the porch. He rang the doorbell. A muted, musical chime sounded. Silence. Maybe nobody would answer.

The door drifted open.

"Hello. Is anybody home?"

With a subtle creak, the door drifted further open.

"I'm coming in. Okay?"

He pushed the door the rest of the way and stopped cold. This was no living room. It was a subterranean cavern, cold and damp. A blue glow beckoned from its depths.

A chill ran through Stephen. *The house can't possibly be this big.*

"Help," echoed. It sounded plaintiff. Real. He breathed deep.

"I'm coming," he shouted. Warmth seeped into him. The Mediums were here. He stepped inside. One foot in front of the other. One step at a time. *One small step for humankind.*

He couldn't tell if he was moving forward or the cave walls stretched inward, shortening and pulling themselves closer like one of those popular trick shots from the movies. The blue glow strengthened. The passageway narrowed until he feared it crush him like a rat in a tin can. He could barely breathe. He wanted to reverse course, but the tunnel seemed even more constrictive behind him. He thought of toothpaste. Would the Mediums lead—no force—him here if it truly risked his life? He had to trust them.

Arms extended, he pushed through a haze of blue glow into a cavernous chamber on the other side. He shuddered. The smell of rancid jelly filled his nose. Gunner Bane stood silhouetted by the strange portal overlooking a street bustling with glowing people.

"So, you've made it," Gunner Bane said. "Welcome to your demise."

"Help me," a voice said. Stephen's eyes drew to an amber pendant hanging from Gunner Bane's neck. A tiny human moved within. Gunner Bane shrugged and touched its surface.

"Oh, that's Mattie, my pet. You have much in common. I believe I have a pendant just your size around here."

"I'm not alone," Stephen said.

"Oh, your friends. I smell them. A bit gassy, if you ask me." Blue-white flames shot from his fingertips. Stephen tensed. The flame was so hot it felt cold, almost frigid.

Energy flowed from his body, forming a shield. And then an arm held the shield. A body attached to the arm.

Styrax. Stephen smiled despite everything. This was his second in command. If he could trust anything to aid him it was his creations.

Styrax pushed forward. Flame parted around the shield. One step, two steps, three steps and he was upon Gunner Bane. The flame ceased.

"You think you've defeated me?" Gunner Bane's body contorted into an amalgamation of monstrous arachnid features. Its proboscis shot out. Styrax smashed it aside. Gunner Bane flailed back. The pendant went flying and shattered into a spray of dust.

"Thank you."

12

Mattie opened his eyes. The lashes were encrusted. He blinked several times to clear his vision. A ceiling came into focus. It was his bedroom, a real ceiling, not the psychedelic he'd experienced for weeks. Is this real? Is any of this real? Did some random dude just barge in and rescue me from Gunner Bane?

He raised his arm. It was surprisingly easy. Still, he felt like he was one-hundred-years old. He wiped grime from his eyes. It was his room. Maybe it was real. He rolled off his bed. Who was that guy? Is he still here? He staggered across the room, knocking a lamp off the shelf in the process, and made his way unsteadily downstairs.

The living room was dingy and dark with cobwebs in the corner. The curtains were drawn, making it completely lifeless. He felt a twinge of guilt. He hadn't cleaned his place in months, ever since his father...

His focus went to the television. It was as dead as the rest of the room. He heard a quiet groan from behind the couch.

"Dad?"

He ran to the noise.

A young man lay on the floor. He was tall and thin with dark hair and round features. It was the guy who saved him.

The man tried to sit up but fell back. Another groan. His eyes were open, but he didn't seem to focus. Mattie hurried to his side.

"It's all right, man. I'm here for you."

13

Stephen sat at the kitchen table. The kitchen was small and old-fashioned, pantry doors leading to the spice rack, an old enamel stove with tall burners.

Mattie brought a platter with a teapot and two cups to the table.

"I hope you like mint tea," he said. "It's all I had handy."

"That's cool." Stephen didn't care about the tea. "What's going on here if you don't mind my asking? That was some weird shit."

"Oh, Gunner. He's the Voice Man's lapdog."

"The Voice Man?"

"A supreme baddie from another dimension."

Stephen went cold. "I know who you mean." Titanos. He didn't dare say it.

Over the next hour, they bonded like brothers. Mattie told him about his cancer, the sickness, the disease. Stephen showed Mattie his artwork on his cellphone and explained how the

Mediums wanted him to create an army.

"I'm in," Mattie said.

ᚦ

Stephen went home with renewed purpose. He would create an army. He and Mattie would destroy Titanos.

He was soon into his third drawing, a creature inspired by the man he'd seen coming out of the flames of the Moran farm on television. It wasn't a man in his illustration, but a dinosaur with mechanical arms and long shredder claws.

I'll call him Claw.

ᚦ

The silhouette of a tremendous throne stood against a backdrop of swirling galaxies and red and purple nebula.

Claw appeared from the side, dragging Gunner Bane by the collar of his cape. Gunner Bane flailed and thrashed, but it had no effect on the monster.

"I've done what you asked," Claw growled. He threw Gunner Bane towards the throne. Gunner Bane sprawled across the jagged black floor.

"Here's your snack."

Dark liquid welled from Gunner Bane's cheek.

"Master, I beg you. Look at all I've done for you."

Titanos leaned into the light. "All you've done," he roared, and the whole world vibrated. "Making the humans aware of my presence. Allowing the Mediums to guess my purpose."

"No, no. I've only done what you ordered."

With a sour scowl, Claw flicked his hand forward. Gunner Bane's head spun into the darkness.

Black liquid pulsed from the stump. Titanos grabbed the heap that had been Gunner Bane and shoved it into his gaping mouth. He chewed twice and swallowed. He wiped his mouth with the back of his arm.

"I trust you will serve me better, Joshua."

14

Eric merged his SUV onto 376. The past month had been a blur of conferences from Denver to San Antonio to Louisiana. He looked forward to the day when he sold enough Xerox contracts to sit back and have a normal life. *Whatever that is.*

A billboard depicted a teen girl reading a book. The slogan read, "A new world awaits…read." The background showed a fantastic, troll-like creature. It reminded him of an illustration Stephen had done for one of his books.

"Stephen." *I should have followed up with him.*

He'd gone out of his way to act normal during their last get together, but Eric knew something was wrong. He hadn't earned a degree in psychology for nothing. The machines he sold were complex, but nothing like people.

I should call him. No, it's on the way, I'll just stop by. He glanced out the side window. Flowers were starting to bloom. It was a sunny day. What a great day to visit an old friend, have a drink or two. *I should stop and pick up some Dogfish Heads.* The fatigue of a busy month lifted.

ᛈ

Jay paused his iPhone XI. One of his students turned the test packet over on his desk. He sighed and set the phone down. The monster with the starfish head glared up at him. *Yeah, well Revolutionary War comes first. Kids gotta learn.*

He walked to the student's desk. He started to pick up the package. On the back page was a monster eerily similar to the starfish creature from *Stranger Things*. But it wasn't quite the same. It looked more like one of Stephen's drawings.

Jay gazed at the student. "Have you been spying on me?"

The kid blinked behind thick glasses. He had long, wavy dark hair that fell down to his shoulders.

"Mr. Beshero, you didn't say we couldn't draw."

"No, Axel. It's ok. Nice work."

He picked up the packet and went back to his desk. He couldn't stop thinking of Stephen. How long had it been since they'd gotten together? *I'll stop by after work.*

ᛈ

Stephen slapped papers onto his desk.

"I told you to draw something, Mattie, not copy mine." Stephen admired his drawing of a sauropod, with its characteristically long neck. Unlike the plant eaters of old, this one was weaponized with vicious, sharp teeth and serrated blades along its mechanical neck and tail. Mattie's, by comparison, looked like a stick figure porcupine.

Mattie curled into the fetal position in his chair. "I tried my best. I'm not as good as you."

"The Mediums brought us together for a purpose. You need to try harder." He sighed. "Look, I'm sorry, Mattie, but we don't have time for whining."

"I'm sick."

"I thought you said The Voice Man healed you."

"Yeah, that's where Gunner Bane came from. But he made me sicker too."

There was a knock at the door, followed by the chimes of the doorbell.

"Are you gonna get that?" Mattie said.

"Might as well. We're not making progress here." He stood and walked through the dining room to the front door. He turned the knob. It wasn't locked. What was the point?

Eric stood beaming on the step. "Look who I ran into."

Jay peered over his shoulder. "Hey, Stephen, how's it going, man?"

"Better now," Stephen said. It surprised him, but he really was glad to see them. "Come on in."

15

attie pulled his arms tighter. He felt cold all over. He felt naked. At least when Gunner Bane had him, he was in his own bed with his own sheets and smell.

Something snapped outside. *He's coming.* A lighter crunching sound. *Bones.* He saw movement in the hallway. *Run,* he thought, but his muscles wouldn't work. He started shivering. "Please don't hurt me."

Two men came through the door. They were about his age. One was tall and skinny with thick glasses and a short beard. The other was squatter with a pale, round face. He wore a rumpled, two-piece suit.

"Hey, guys, this is Mattie." Stephen strode into the room. He looked more relaxed. Mattie tried to relax too. *They don't look like demons.*

"How's it going, man?" the tall one said. He extended his hand. "I'm Eric Francis."

Mattie stared at his hand. He wore a smart watch on his wrist. He felt an urge to touch it.

"Don't mind him," Stephen said. "Mattie's been through a lot." He looked at Mattie. "Haven't you?"

Mattie nodded meekly.

"Oh, what happened?" Eric said.

"Just your average demon possession," Stephen said.

Eric's eyes went wide. Stephen slapped him on the shoulder. "I'm just kidding, but it *has* been traumatic."

"Oh, I'm Jay by the way," the shorter one said with a grin.

Mattie remembered Gunner Bane grinning. So many teeth. He drew into himself.

When Mattie emerged again, the three were on the other side of the room. Stephen had wheeled his chair over and Eric and Jay leaned against the wall near a window. They were talking quietly.

Mattie's gaze drifted to the window. There were trees out there, not thick woods, but enough to hide in.

"I heard a noise," he blurted. The others' conversation stopped.

"Welcome back," Eric said. "Stephen's been telling us about your predicament. How long have you been having these episodes?"

"They're not episodes. My dad's dead. My dog's dead. Gunner Bane..." *He's dead too*.

"Look," Eric said, "I'm sorry for your losses. Sometimes tragedy will make us disconnect. Do you think that's what's happening to you?"

"I told them this is real," Stephen said. "I told them about the Mediums, the voice man, everything."

Eric looked skeptical. "You have to admit, man, that sounds a little far-fetched, don't you think?"

"It's not as far-fetched as you think," Jay said. "There's a lot of corollaries in Greek Mythology. This reminds me of when Athena told Perseus to defeat the gorgon Medusa."

"Oh, come on, this is real," Eric said.

"And that wasn't? They fought wars over those events. Gorgon's gaze turned people to stone."

Mattie stood. "Gunner Bane told me saying his master's name would turn me to stone."

"See," Jay said.

Eric shook his head. "You're feeding his delusions."

"Let me show you my drawings," Stephen said. He walked between them to his desk.

16

Eric paged through Stephen's binder. Stephen had always drawn fantasy and comic book characters, but there was something different about them. Each bore a level of hyper detail and violence unusual for Stephen. These weren't cartoonish at all. They were war machines.

"Are you angry about something?" Eric said.

"You mean other than the world being on the brink of destruction?"

"You don't actually believe that, do you?"

"Believe? I know it. I was there. That's what I've been trying to tell you."

Eric pointed at a page. "You know this isn't real, right?"

"Not on the page," Stephen said. "Drawing them helps me make them real here." He pointed to his temple. "There's a war going on in a realm you won't even comprehend."

Eric closed the binder and set it on the desk. "These are very good, Stephen." He glanced at Mattie, curled in his chair. "I have to go now. Something important has come up."

He looked to Jay. "You have to leave too, right?"

Jay looked confused for a moment. "Oh, yeah, that thing. We'll try this again another time."

"But I haven't finished," Stephen said. "I need you guys."

"And you know we'll always be there, right?" Eric said. He tugged Jay's elbow. "We'll show ourselves out."

They walked briskly through the hallway. "What's this about?" Jay said.

"Wait till we're outside."

As soon as Jay shut the door behind them, he turned to Eric. "Ok, spill it."

"I'm worried," Eric said. "Didn't you see those drawings?"

"He's always drawing wild shit," Jay said.

"Not like this. I think he really believes in this war of his."

"Well there is a historical precedent," Jay said.

"Shut it, Jay. This is not some academic conference. This is our friend."

"Ok, well what do you propose we do?"

"I know a doctor I want to talk to and maybe get a referral for Stephen."

"He'll never go."

"You got a better idea?"

"Maybe I can do some research at the library, show him where these ideas come from. Once he sees they're derivative, he'll let it go."

"Sounds like a plan. Let's get going. I'll call you later."

"Excuse us, gentlemen. May we have a moment of your time?" Eric's heart jumped. Two men wearing three-piece black suits and top hats approached. They seemed very tan for this time of year.

"Not a good time," Jay said.

One of the men extended a thick book. The binding was black leather, the pages edged in black. *That's no bible,* Eric thought. The other man read from the open page in a deeply resonant voice.

"Before this reality, there was an infinitude. At its center, a being of such omnipotence, omniscience and omnipresence, that all the flows and eddies that would give life bowed before him. Their very essence quivered in His presence. None dared utter his name. Nor do we."

"What does this have to do with us?" Jay said. He pushed between the two. The speaker turned with him and made a jabbing motion with his fist. Jay grunted and fell to his knees, then toppled forward.

The speaker turned to Eric. "And you?"

Eric raised his hand defensively. "Jay?" Something pinched his neck. He felt himself falling too.

17

Jay came to. Everything was dark. His hands were bound behind him. He tried to stand but his ankles were bound too. *Where am I?*

He couldn't say it. His mouth was taped. His back was sore where the strange man had punched him. His head hurt. He tasted blood. He felt woozy as if Novocain was wearing off.

I'm blind, he thought. Then he thought of Eric. *Did they kill him? Did he escape?* He grunted as loud as he could. They were moving. A bounce caused a spike of pain throughout his body.

He leaned, trying to feel for Eric. The vehicle jounced again. He toppled sideways onto something soft.

"Hey!"

Eric, Jay thought.

"Get him up," a voice said. Hands grabbed roughly and pulled him back to a sitting position. Cloth twisted around his face. His nose stung. It must be a hood. That thought brought some relief.

The momentum shifted. The van must be turning. A few minutes later, there was a squeal of brakes. He almost fell over in the opposite direction.

The van stopped. Doors clunked. Footsteps came around the side. Hinges squealed. Jay felt light flood over him.

"Bring them inside." He recognized the voice of the man who had read from the book. Hands grabbed his feet. A quick snick and the bonds parted. The blade scraped his calf. *Hey, watch it,* he tried to say, but he was already being dragged from the van by another set of hands. His feet hit asphalt and he stumbled into a well-muscled arm.

"Careful. We do not wish to be noticed in this world."

He heard another set of feet hit the asphalt. Someone else jumped down and guided him to the left. It was hard to walk. The person beside him had to support him.

They stepped up to a sidewalk. His companion shoved him up a slight incline. "Keep moving."

I can't even see where I'm going.

"You don't want to see where you're going, friend."

A door opened. Warm air brushed his hood. Now he was on a smooth floor. Footsteps echoed. He tried to count how many, but it was impossible. All he could determine was that there was a mix of dress shoes and sneakers.

"Take them through there," the leader said. He heard a squealing hinge. Another door clunked open and he was pushed through. Even with the hood he could feel space constricting around him.

"Down you go," his captor said. He turned him to the right. "Watch your step."

Jay felt tentatively for the first step and eased his way down one stair at a time. He counted twelve in total. They pushed him through a room. His hip brushed a filing cabinet. He heard a snick and a sliding sound. His captor forced him ahead and the ground suddenly sloped downward.

How deep does this go? He thought of the underground maze where ancient Greeks sacrificed people to the Minotaur. He wanted to see what it looked like. He wished they'd take his hood off.

The floor leveled. His captor pulled him to a stop.

The hood ripped from his head. He blinked. There was barely enough light to see two cages shaped like bullets, hardly large enough for a man to stand in.

His captor shoved him into the first cage. "Put your hands here."

Jay frowned, trying to make sense of the command. He turned and saw a scrawny man in street clothes. The knife in his hand wasn't scrawny. The blade must have been six inches long. *He's going to kill me.*

"Don't you want your hands freed?"

Jay grudgingly extended his bound wrists and closed his eyes. He felt a quick slice and the zip tie parted.

A silver chain hung from the man's neck. It ended in a silver circle containing a Nordic symbol. *Thurisaz.*

Jay ripped the duct tape from his mouth. "Is that the mark of thorn?" The rune was from the age of giants and represented chaos incarnate.

The man shrugged and turned away. In the other cage, a similarly dressed man cut Eric's bonds. Eric looked traumatized.

He didn't even try to remove the duct tape but slouched into the bars and slid down to a seated position.

18

Stephen grabbed another drawing from Mattie.

"You still don't get it. You're just copying. Try again."

Mattie pressed pen to paper and began drawing robotically. Stephen stared out the window. How was he going to defeat The Voice Man if he couldn't even get Mattie on board?

He squinted. "Wait a minute. Is that Eric's car? He left a half hour ago."

Maybe he went with Jay. But no, Jay's silver Mercury Milan was right behind it.

"Something's wrong. Come on, we gotta go."

Mattie didn't move. The pen continued to draw.

"Didn't you hear me?" He shook Mattie's shoulders.

The image taking form depicted a rounded cage.

"Why are you drawing…" He saw a face. "Is that Jay? Where is this coming from?"

Mattie dropped the pen. "I see them." He pointed to his head.

"Them?" Stephen said.

"Your friends."

ᚦ

Stephen pulled on the door handle of the black SUV. Of course, it was locked. Eric always locked his car.

He walked to the silver Mercury Milan and tried it. The door swung open. In the passenger seat was a brown leather briefcase. Stephen leaned across and unsnapped the clasps. it made a crisp *click, click*.

"They're in a dark place," Mattie said.

"Do you know where? Can you draw it?"

"It's moving images, not a still picture. Security camera, maybe."

"But where? How are we gonna find out where?"

"A church," Mattie said. "I see pews. An altar. I'm going outside now." His eyes squeezed tight. "Saint Joseph the Worker. The sign is peeling."

"I know where that is," Stephen said. "Let's go."

"No, they say you should prepare," Mattie said.

"Who says?" Stephen said. *The Mediums.* "Prepare what?"

"Your army."

19

Eric thought of Taylor. It was late May and they were to be married in October. What would she do without him? He thought of her laugh and beautiful smile. She was like the sun rising when she walked into a room.

"Come on, buck up, Eric," Jay said. "We'll get outta here."

"No, we won't," Eric said. "We're dead."

"Why didn't they kill us already?" Jay said. "Why did they bother to blindfold us. It's obviously ransom."

"Well, they're gonna be disappointed," Eric said. "I'm in debt up to my eyeballs. Weddings are expensive."

"Yeah, I got one coming up myself," Jay said.

"Why us?" Eric said. "We're not worth anything."

"Do you think it's what Stephen said?"

"You mean his fantasy world of comic book soldiers and conspiracy plots?"

"It's not so far out there. Look at Scientology. It's all about aliens—Thetan's, they call em. That's a Greek base, you know?"

"Enough already. Just stop."

"All I'm saying is millions of people believe in this stuff. Keep an open mind. People are motivated by all kinds of shit."

"Shut up," Eric said.

"All I'm…"

"Quiet. Do you hear that?"

A quiet whirring sounded. His eyes tracked to a red LED across the corridor. It was a security camera, and it was swiveling between the two of them. He stood. The cage was barely high enough.

"We're being watched," Eric said.

Jay stared at the camera. "They're probably just keeping an eye on us."

"What if someone hacked into the system?"

"Who's the optimist now?" Jay said.

20

Mattie peered through the hedge bordering the church property. A sign stood near the sidewalk before the entrance.

SAINT JOSEPH THE WORKER CATHOLIC PARISH.

Sure enough, the sign was peeling.

"Now we're cooking with gas," Stephen said. "What else do you see?"

"Front door," Mattie said. He focused on the glass doors. The empty vestibule beyond was carpeted with a floral design. "The coast is clear."

"I can see that for myself," Stephen said. "I mean do you see anything in your mind?"

"No, it's gone."

"I guess we gotta go inside."

They made their way to the doors. Stephen tried one. It was unlocked. He looked tentatively at Mattie. "This is too easy. They could be expecting us."

"I think something's helping us."

"I hope you're right."

He pulled the door and hey crept inside. "Careful. They probably have security."

Corridors on either side of the vestibule led to the chapel. Mattie felt an uplifting sensation. He hadn't been to church since his mother died 21 years ago. After the darkness of recent events, this felt like light.

Stephen walked ahead. "We're looking for the basement," he said. The chapel was long and sloped. Rows of pews descended to a raised platform holding the altar. Gold and silver chalices gleamed. A candelabra was lit. Light flickered across a larger than life crucifix attached to the wall.

Mattie felt an urge to go to his knees and pray.

"Crap." Stephen pointed to a security camera. A red light blinked.

Mattie frowned and the light extinguished.

"Does it mean it's off?" Stephen said.

"I think so."

"Come on, hurry," Stephen said.

"We have to give thanks," Mattie said. "Someone is watching over us."

"There's no time." He tugged Mattie's arm.

"Thank you," Mattie whispered on their way past the altar.

A glass door opened into a wider hall. They came to another security camera. The red light went out.

"You're right, Mattie. Somebody is watching out for us."

Mattie nodded happily. "We're not alone."

They came to another room. Light poured through a bank of Florida ceiling windows, illuminating a mural of The Last Supper. Across the room a metal door was marked NO EXIT.

"I bet that goes to the basement," Stephen said.

Mattie gazed into the brown eyes of the Jesus depicted on the wall. One eye winked. "It does," Mattie said.

They descended concrete steps to a small, empty room. *Now what?* Mattie took a folded page from his pocket. It was the picture he had drawn of Jay in the cage.

Jay's lips moved. Mattie pressed the paper to his ear. "Straight ahead. There's a latch."

Mattie moved his palms along the cloth-covered wall until he felt a depression. He pushed the tapestry aside, revealing a decorative plate. A symbol marked its center, a vertical line with an inverted triangle.

He pushed the plate. There was no give.

"See how the wall's scuffed?" Stephen said. "Try turning it."

Mattie cupped the plate in his palm and twisted. A click sounded and a section of the wall pushed in and slid sideways. Dank air flowed from the opening. Stephen went through first. Mattie squinted into the dimness. The cages were exactly as he'd seen them in his head.

"Dude," Jay said. "You're a sight for sore eyes."

Thank you, Mattie thought.

"Careful, they're watching," Eric said. He pointed through the bars. As Mattie stepped through the opening, that camera went dead, too.

Jay rattled his cage. "You got the key, man?"

"Key?" Stephen said.

"What kind of half-assed rescue is this?" Jay said.

"Do you know how to pick locks?" Eric said.

"Not a clue."

Mattie found a rusted crowbar against the wall behind Eric's cage. He inserted the flat end between the hasp and the lock body and pushed down with as much leverage as he could muster. Metal scraped.

"They'll hear you," Eric said.

A Gregorian chant sounded through the door.

"Must be their evening programming," Jay said.

"Oh, it's more than that," Stephen said. "Trust me. We are not in this alone."

Part of the padlock clattered to the floor. Mattie handed the crowbar to Stephen.

21

The Throne of Ultimate Chaos pulsed. Atria and ventricles fluttered and flexed as trying to break free of the tumor that formed the base. Titanos sensed a new force in the microcosm, and this disturbed him. He didn't like the emotion. It was something lesser gods experienced. It should not exist in his reality.

He glared at the bone-strewn floor. Horned skulls, spiked tails, armored plates, a prodigious assortment. Those pesky humans would consider these creatures monsters of great power. To Him, they were carpeting. And yet the humans continued to vex him. No doubt this was their doing. How he didn't know. Something had escaped him. Something had slipped from his grasp.

"Unacceptable," he roared.

He gripped his weapon. The bones of his hand pressed through his hide. Veins protruded from his inner arms. This was anger, this was rage. *This* was an emotion he was familiar with.

He stood from the Throne and strode toward the nexus. Bones crunched beneath his feet. A mist of calcium danced and settled as he passed.

The humans would soon regret crossing him.

Book Three:

Universal Armageddon

1

my looked over the DVD cover for *Law Abiding Citizen*.
The split frame depicted a stern-looking Gerard Butler
on the top pane and Jamie Fox looking defiant from the
bottom. She'd been waiting to see this movie for a while.

"That's a great movie," Jen said.

Amy nodded. She liked Gerard Butler in the role of vengeance-
seeking victim of justice. The problem was she had just paid her
cable bill and didn't have any splurge money.

"Too bad Stephen's not here," Brian said. "He likes this
place."

"Yeah," Amy said. "I called him. He seemed a little…
distracted."

"There's always next time," Jen said.

Amy reluctantly put the case back on the rack. She worried
about Stephen. He didn't sound like himself on the phone. He'd
gone into his creative cocoons in the past, but this was different.
He seemed agitated. Maybe she would call him later.

"Let's go catch a bite," Brian said. "I gotta get back to work."

"Yeah, me too," Jen said.

Amy sighed. "Back to the fourth grade from hell."

As they left, a box caught her eye. It was large, almost huge. Titanis beckoned in bold, blocky letters. A gleaming red eye glinted from the box's cellophane window. The creature inside was a mechanized brontosaurus. Cameron had been begging for this toy for a month. Her son was going through a stage. Monster trucks and monster monsters.

She looked into the red eye and it looked into her. She shivered. That was the last toy she was going to buy her son.

"What's wrong?" Jen said.

"Nothing. Just a feeling."

"Someone walked over your grave," Brian said with a laugh.

"Actually, yes," Amy said.

"The horror section will do that to you." Brian pushed through the glass door. It was sunny outside.

2

avid pressed the doorbell. A muffled chime sounded in Stephen's house.

"You think he's home?" Ezzy said. She shifted the ice cream cake to her hip and reached with her free hand for the buzzer.

"I just rang it," David said. "Two is overkill." He glanced at the box in his free hand, a sculpt of Pennywise from *IT*. Very detailed. Very professional. *I should have wrapped it.*

"We could have had the party at home," Ezzy said.

"Well, you know that won't work. Stephen's fighting with Dad again."

"We'll bring the party to him," Ezzy said.

"Thank you, Miss Obvious."

"What if he's not here? The cake's melting."

"That's his car. Where's he gonna go without his car?"

"He has friends."

David raised an eyebrow. "This is Stephen we're talking about, right?"

The door cracked open. An unfamiliar eye glared out. "What do you want?"

"Where's Stephen?" David said. "Who are you?"

"It's Stephen's birthday," Ezzy said. "We brought a cake."

The eye shifted to the cake. "I don't know. He's pretty busy."

"Tell him his brother and sister are here," David said.

"I had a family once." The door closed.

"What now?" Ezzy said. "Should we call the police?"

The door opened again. Stephen stood there.

"Hey guys. This isn't the best time,"

"Of course it is," Ezzy said. "It's your birthday, Greenman."

"Oh, I forgot." Stephen moved aside. "Come in."

"How could you forget your birthday?" David said. He brushed past Stephen into the living room. It was dark, curtains drawn. The smell struck him hard, an old library overflowing with moldy paper. He didn't say anything.

"What kind of cake?"

David's focus went to the kitchen archway. The strange man that had opened the door stood there stiffly. Hair stood from his silhouette like Frankenstein's bride post-electrocution. Sloping shoulders accentuated his long neck.

"Don't mind Mattie," Stephen said. "He's had a tough year."

David forced a friendly smile before returning his attention to his brother. "What's up? It's like a morgue in here."

Ezzy marched across the living room, nudged Mattie aside, and set the cake on the kitchen table. The light came on.

"Paper plates, Stephen? The stack in the sink is dirty and I'm not washing."

David patted Stephen's shoulder. "That's our sister. Some things never change."

"*Thank God,*" Stephen muttered. "Can we use paper towels?"

"It's ice cream. Keep up, Stephen." The sound of running water drowned out her voice.

David shoved the package into Stephen's midsection. "Here's your present, Bro."

Stephen looked startled. "What is...a clown? Oh, oh, Pennywise. You shouldn't have. It must have cost you a pretty... uh, penny."

David laughed. "Pun noted. Don't worry. I got a deal."

"Thanks," Stephen said. "Let's get some cake."

ᛈ

David watched Mattie gulp down a second piece of cake. He dragged his fingers through the puddle and licked them noisily. David's appetite vanished.

"So, what's the deal with your friend?" he said. "He's got the table manners of a Neanderthal. Does he even know how to use a fork?"

"Stop being so judgmental," Ezzy said. "Can't you see the poor man's been through a trauma? He might even be anemic. Is he receiving care?"

"I watch out for him," Stephen said.

"I mean professional. Does he see a doctor?"

"Leave it be," Stephen said. "There's too much going on right now."

Ezzie touched Mattie's hand. "Would you like come coffee or tea?" He stared at her hand for a second before nodding.

"I need to show you something," Stephen said to David. He pushed his chair out and stood.

"Sure," David said. He stood too and followed Stephen to his bedroom. The first thing he noticed was the clutter. Clothes strewn across the floor. Trash bags overflowing with wadded up paper. An unkempt cot was set up in the far corner, more like a nest than a bed. *That must be where his new roommate sleeps.*

"I hope you have tornado insurance," David said.

"It's here," Stephen said. He tapped his desk. It was a detailed drawing. It looked like the dilophosaurus from *Jurassic Park*, a fierce and toothy lizard with an oozing tongue, spiny features, decorative frill and hyper-detailed floral and marbled patterns on its scaly skin.

"I call him *Dimorphodon*," Stephen said. "Titanos destroyer."

"You see your problem, don't you?" David said.

3

Stephen examined the drawing more closely. "It looks perfectly fine to me. I've been working on it for two days straight."

"Look at that frill," David said. "Is it made of gossamer? That wouldn't protect you from a stick. It would be like trying to defend your most vulnerable extremities with a potato chip."

"But look at the bright green, blue, yellow and red," Stephen said. "See how this pattern is repeated here? It's all about balance."

"Sure, it'll look great on a shelf," David said, "but on't last two seconds in battle."

Cold water splashed over Stephen. *He's right. What am I thinking? Letting the artist get in the way of the strategist. We have a battle to win. This is war.*

Stephen plopped onto his chair and started sketching a blue metal plate to frame the head. It would need hinges, bio-hinges… "Here." He jabbed the pencil point down. "And here, and here."

Some time later he looked up. "What do you think, David?" His brother was nowhere to be seen. Stephen sat still for a moment. He sighed. When he turned to the window, it was dark outside.

He stood and exited his office. He could still show Mattie his new and improved work. At least someone would appreciate the effort. "Mattie," he called, but Mattie didn't answer.

He found his broken friend hunched over the kitchen sink, picking crumbs off a stack of plates. He pushed his revised drawing between Mattie and the the sink. "What do you think?"

Mattie stared. Stephen couldn't tell if he was confused or in a state of admiration. "Nice," he finally said.

4

David was disturbed by Stephen's behavior. The look on Ezzy's face said she was concerned too. *We need to do something,* he thought.

He fixed his gaze on the road ahead. "Jay and Eric are his best friends," he said. "And Jay only lives a block away. Shouldn't we at least try to talk to him?"

Ezzy shifted in the passenger seat. "Mom and Dad are expecting us for dinner. She'll be tossing the salad now."

"I'm always late," David said. "They won't blame you." He gave her a sideways grin.

Ezzy looked uncertain.

"Come on," David said. "You know he needs our help."

"Again," she whispered.

"Again." David gripped the steering wheel. "He's our brother, Ezz."

"Accident of birth," Ezzy muttered. She gazed through the side window.

David guided them into the turn lane. "You know I'm right." He waited for an oncoming semi, then turned onto the side road leading to Jay's. "Mom's salad is overrated anyway."

Ezzy laughed. "You guys didn't plan all this out just to avoid your having to eat something healthy, did you?"

David shrugged and grinned. "There's a silver lining in every sow's ear, Sis." That was one of his father's sayings.

A few minutes later, they parked in front of Jay's house. They got out and David knocked on the door. When Jay answered. David was surprised to see Eric on the sofa. He wasn't aware that they knew each other outside their friendship with Stephen.

"What's up?" Jay said.

"We need to talk about Stephen."

"Sure," Jay said. "Come in." He gestured toward an overstuffed chair. David waited for Ezzy to sit, then perched on the cushioned arm beside her.

"What's going on?" Jay said. "Did something else happen?"

Something else? David glanced to Ezzy. She gripped his forearm lightly.

"He's living like a recluse," David said, "and he has a roommate with the mentality of a feral child."

"It's worse than you know," Eric said. "We believe he's fallen in with a cult." Jay nodded.

Ezzy's grip on his arm tightened. "Why would you say that?" she said through clenched teeth.

"They took us as leverage," Jay said. "We barely escaped by the skin of our teeth. If it wasn't for Stephen and Mattie we'd still be in a dungeon."

"Mattie?" David said. "The weird roommate? He belongs in a cult if you ask me."

"We have to stage an intervention," Eric said.

"Are you serious?" Jay said. "Interventions are for drugs."

"He's obviously in a toxic situation. We need to get him out."

"Count me in," David said.

"Count us in," Ezzy said, and released David's forearm. David felt immediately guilty for not including her.

"When?" Jay said. "How?"

"There's no time like the present," Eric said. "Interventions work best when there's a number of advocates. Does he have other friends or family?"

"Yeah,," Ezzy said. "Believe it or not. I'll Amy, Jen and Brian."

5

Stephen glanced from face to face. David stood behind the sofa where Ezzy was comforting Mattie. Jay and Eric had pulled chairs from the kitchen. Brian claimed the rocking chair leaving, the loveseat for Amy and Jen. Everyone stared expectantly.

"What's the occasion, guys?" He tried to sound casual, but even he recognized the tension in his voice. This wasn't good.

"You know we're your friends," David said. "Right?"

"We're doing this out of love," Ezzy said.

"What are you talking about?"

"We've noticed some disturbing things," David said. "You disappear for days at a time…"

"I've always been that way," Stephen said. "I'm an artist."

"Not like this," Ezzy said. "And what about him?" She looked to Mattie. "No offense."

"What am I supposed to do," Stephen said, "put him on the street?"

"This is not normal," David said. "We're here to help you."

"Both," Ezzy added with a reassuring smile. Mattie looked flummoxed. He glanced nervously to Stephen.

"These are not normal times," Stephen said. "There's bigger things going on."

"Sometimes," Eric said, "stress can detach us from our experience."

Stephen felt the room closing in. "You don't believe me? I'll show you." He hurried to his bedroom. He rifled through the sketches covering his desk and nearly ran back to the living room, a drawing stretched between his hands.

"This is Titan…" A cold sweat came over him. Even thinking the name was disturbing.

"Dude, that's a drawing," Jay said. " It's not real."

"Of course it's not real. You don't want to meet the real thing, believe me."

"This may be worse than we thought," Eric said.

Amy stood and touched Stephen's shoulder. It was like an electric shock. He jolted away from her, down the hall to his bedroom.. "You don't understand." *You don't understand.*

"You don't understand!" Mattie shrieked.

Stephen sorted through piles of mostly-finished drawings. Radon was a giant feathered bird capable of supersonic flight that leaves a trail of destruction in its wake. Aeron was a mechanical jet capable of leveling cities with its laser-guided missiles. A third drawing surfaced. This one depicted a ghostly ninja bearing an exaggerated scythe and axe.

He carried these creations to the other room, unsure of why he did this. Why would his friends believe these drawings when they hadn't believed the first one? He had to try. He moved to the center of the circle of doubters.

"This is Radon," he said, turning slowly. "He is the primitive force that has terrified and protected us for as long as man as existed." He met Amy's eyes, hoping to find some spark of belief. All he found was pity. The only person who believed him was Mattie, and that didn't count.

He shifted the second drawing to the front. "This is Aeron. It comes from Ganymeade through a dimensional portal from the future."

Mattie started quivering. "It's a one, two punch," he said. Ezzy grasped his forearm.

"And this is Ghastonia," Stephen said. "He's a revenant from the shadowy death realm where our enemy resides. A source of great wisdom and deadly power."

David reached out. "Sounds like the makings of a killer graphic novel, Brother. But that's not why we're here."

"This is happening," Stephen said. "It *is* real. How do I make you see?"

"It's okay," Amy said. "We're here for you."

"Can't you at least *try* to believe? Can't you give me that much? Look at this sketch. Try to imagine it as real as you or me. The drawing's not real, but what inspired it is." He saw frowns and confusion, but at least they were looking.

A whisper sounded. "Stephen speaks truly."

"Did that drawing just fucking move?" Jay said.

Stephen glanced down. Ghastonia's scythe was now pointed toward the audience. As he watched, the axe slowly shifted until the two weapon shafts crossed. That was Ghastonia's signature move before battle.

A gasp hissed through the room. Jen bolted to her feet. "No!" Her face was rigid. The whites of her eyes gleamed. Fear spiked through Stephen. She had the same aggressive posture as The Voice Man.

She blinked and her eyes were normal again. "Listen," she said. Words appeared in the air as if being scribed by a quill in rich, black ink.

Nightmares in The Fourth Dimension

"Is anybody else seeing this?" Stephen said.

"Seeing what?" Eric said. "I'm hearing music. It's dark and dense. I feel alone."

"Yeah," Jay said. "I see some dude in a warehouse. He's writing something. It's like a movie."

"Made for TV movie," Amy said. "I'm waiting for a commercial. And what's up with that hokey 70's music soundtrack?"

"Hokey?" Eric said. "It's classical. It's textured."

"It's an aural story," Jen said. "He's speaking words from his journal. It makes me want to do a podcast."

"This is the intro-level map," Brian said.

"It's a sketch to me," David said. "Like flashcards."

We're experiencing the same thing differently, Stephen thought. *This must be how the Mediums intersect with us.*

Words continued to appear.

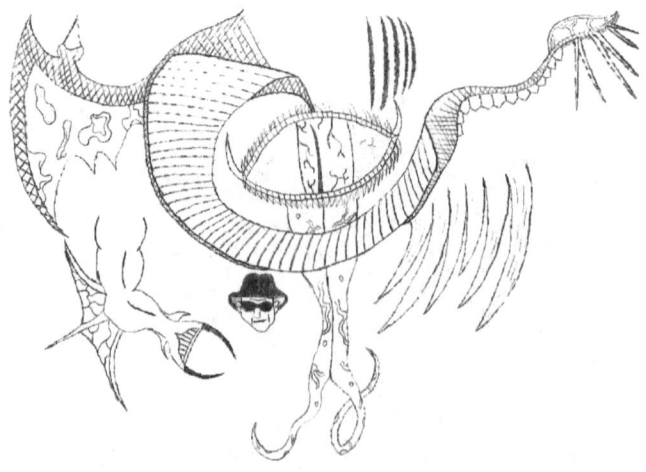

...It's too dark and cold in here for my taste.

My name is Howard Steven Gram; I am thirty years old and a former grad student. I studied in the Department of Earth and Environmental Science, University of Pennsylvania. It felt as surreal as anything could have possibly felt, to be in a grad program at such a prestigious (at least for western Pennsylvania) school of vertebrate paleontology.

Ever since I was a boy, hell, not even a boy, but a toddler I had an infatuation that some may call unhealthy, with dinosaurs and prehistoric life in general. It was an obsession that trailed me into young adulthood like the most conspicuous stalker you would ever want to encounter. It refused to go away. That's how I ended up where I did.

My mother bought me a placemat during a period when most children can only utter mommy or da-da. On the front was a beautifully detailed portrait of the animals I would grow to love, lumbering about in their natural habitat. I ate breakfast, lunch and dinner admiring that wonderful scene.

But there was the other side of the placemat. Although the side that I've already described, the side on which I dined, was rather aesthetically pleasing to my young eye, the opposite side enraptured me even more. The educational side included information about each dinosaur depicted on the placemat. The pictures of them were dead ringers for the depictions from the other side. They were naturally drawn by the same artist. Beside these miniature works of art were tidbits of information presented in bullet point format.

Categories such as name, height, length, weight, era in which the animal lived, whether they were herbivorous or carnivorous, etcetera. Some were piscivores, which meant they persisted on fish. Piscivores included dinosaurs such as Suchomimus, Baryonyx, Irritator, and the largest theropod we know of, Spinosaurus Aegyptiacus. There is no evidence, at least within the fossil record, of any dinosaur belonging to any clade being actively omnivorous like Kodiak, brown, black or grizzly bears. Although it stood to reason to my hungry mind that some dinosaurs may have exhibited this behavior on rare occasions.

There was a flying dinosaur included in this rather eclectic group, many of which didn't even live in the same time period. Looking back, I suppose they were grouped together for just the reason of being eclectic. This dinosaur was the only flying dinosaur that ever lived, and no, it wasn't the pterodactyl. Members from the genus *pterosaurs*, such as pterodactyls, weren't dinosaurs, but flying reptiles.

This dinosaur's name was Archaeopteryx. When I read the name I pronounced it correctly. There wasn't a syllable that suffered from mispronunciation. I don't recall this, but my uncle Francis supposedly damn near fell off his chair.

Ever since that day, Uncle Francis suggested I be tested to see if I had genius-level intellect. Between my advanced lexicon, knowledge of dinosaurs and prehistoric life in general, as well as my seemingly eidetic memory, it was accepted that I might be classified as such. Alas, this view was not shared by my colleagues in the scientific community.

According to my mother, I was a rather precocious child. The fact that names such as Archaeopteryx and Rhamphorhynchus (my favorite of the pterosaurs) rolled off my tongue without the assistance of bracketed groups of syllables you through each step, helped to solidify this. estimation

In addition to bestowing upon me a predilection for excavating fossils buried for eons beneath beds of rock, my first placemat instilled within me a love of the printed page. It required me to read in order to discover. I've always preferred that verb to 'learn'.'Discover' is such a broader, vaster, all-encompassing terminology more befitting the infinite cosmos. If you were engaged in the act of discovering instead of learning, you were onto something much bigger. During expeditions, even under the proper supervision of our instructors and funders, I thrived on that moment of discovery, that breath-stealing, heart stalling excitement. You think that you live for those moments. That is, until the ugly truth is revealed.

Initially, we weren't sure what we were looking at. Allow me to clear that comment up a bit. We *did* know exactly what we were looking at. It was a femur, or thighbone, of a dinosaur whose proportions were immense beyond anything a paleontologist had seen. This was significant. No dinosaur remotely close to this size had been discovered in the western region of the keystone state. The dinosaurs that did live in this area were comparable in size to Troodon or Compsognathus, the little guys that probably couldn't harm a grown man,unless they formed a pack.

From an evolutionary standpoint, those two predators would have been the main contenders amongst the terrible lizards to evolve into humanoids had the great Cretaceous-Tertiary event not killed them off. But I digress.

This was an earth-shattering find. Not only was this the first of its kind in what I think was the most beautiful state in the nation, but it was also the largest of its kind. We believed we were viewing the fossilized femur of a sauropod, the largest terrestrial organisms in the history of our world. To the layperson, these were dinosaurs with giraffe-like necks, although they are more closely related to elephants. Archetypical *Brontosaurus* comes to mind. was making a scientific comeback. After its discovery, it was eventually atrributed to the genus *Apatosaurus*, but recent findings suggested enough differences to warrant its own title. And how could anyone forget the legendary Diplodocus when thinking of the unique sauropod taxon?

My peers and professor excavated this momentous scientific gift, certain to baffle paleontologists worldwide. We had mistaken it for the femur of a long-necked animal, probably due in part to the suggestion my professor (who also funded our expeditions and provided the paychecks) since they were the only animalshe knew of that reached such astronomical proportions. There were giants among the sauropods known as Titanosaurs, but they were relegated to South America

In truth, I deserved credit for the find. I bit my tonue and worked my trowel with the rest of crew, but inside I knew. The only reason we happened upon our discovery was because I'd typed the wrong coordinates into my Global Positioning System unit.

My mind was blown clean from my skull upon discovering the bone was hollow. To somebody not well versed in paleontology, bones that are hollowed out like exoskeletons don't mean much. To geeks like me, it meant everything, because such bones are characteristic of theropods, meat-eating dinosaurs, including velociraptor and Tyrannosaurus Rex. Modern birds inherited this trait from their carnivorous ancestors.

That wasn't the only feature indicative of a predator. Ridges in the bone itself were characteristic the femurs of theropods. Known as the Fourth Trochantors these areas for attachment in which the tendons and ligaments of the thigh connect.

Without a degree in hand, I had become the envy of paleontologists worldwide. That's what Dr. Balm told me, and I believed him. All because of a typing error. Who would have thought that a simple mistake could lead to the find of a lifetime? They say that history likes to repeat itself. As cliched as that sounds, I have come to find it to be rather true. It was under identical circumstances—typing the wrong latitude and longitude into a GPS—that another of the largest dinosaurs of all, Paralitian, was discovered.

At the time, I thought to myself, *wow, what a coincidence.* How little I knew then.

þ

When a new dinosaur is discovered, dinosaur fanatics like me are usually the only people to know about it. This time was different. No longer was I just a dinosaur nerd on the outside looking in, I was a member of the actual community I'd yearned to be a part of for so long. I didn't actually receive fame or recognition. Paleontologists rarely do. Think about it. How many paleontologists can the average person can name?

None of that mattered to me, not at all. I shied from the limelight. What I was most looking forward to, was logging onto my laptop and exploring major search engines such as Yahoo, Bing and Google. For as long as I've been online, major scientific headlines and articles were always displayed on prominent websites. Every time a new "terrible lizard" was brought to light by teams of scientists, regardless of how big or small it may have been, there was at least one major write up to be found somewhere. I was shocked when I opened my laptop, signed on, and found that there wasn't a single publication.

After they'd made a plaster cast of the bone and extracted the ginormous chunk of earth in which it was encased, the bone, now very personal to me, was supposedly auctioned for several million on the black market. It was truly a shame. In fact, it made me nauseated. I hoped and prayed it was purchased by another paleontologist, somebody would study it and learn from it as much as they admired it, and who would use it to inform the world. Alas, that wasn't to be the case.

History tends to be recycled. This wasn't the first time fossils had been auctioned at private events. Stolen from scientific minds by greedy corporate interests only stored in the dark in some warehouse, leaving the rest of us to recall it through haphazardly scribbled notes and low-quality photographs.

You may have heard of a dinosaur named *Amphicoelias Fragillimus*. It is one of the more obscure species, though it belonged to the same family as Diplodocus. If size estimates are correct, this creature would have been the largest dinosaur on record. Measuring 198 feet in length, and weighing up to 135 short tons, this animal would have been a sight unlike any other. Its femur alone was estimated to be between twelve and thirteen feett, possibly up to fifteen feet. Anyway, that's the fate that this amazing animal was relegated to, making knowledge hard to acquire even amongst people who had worked in the field for years. My specimen was bigger and *predatory*, multiple times the size of the largest meat eater that we knew.

I wasn't prepared to passively watch as some secretive thief snatched away what I'd literally dreamed of for years. And for what? All for a pocketful of cash to squander. What bothered me most was that nobody, Dr. Balm included, seemed to know what happed after the fossil was crated off. It was almost as if it had fallen into a black hole or abyss, some vortex of forgetfulness. People around me pretended they didn't know what I was talking about when I asked if experts had managed to acquire the item. They simply repeated ad nausea that it was purchased by an anonymous rich collector who wished to remain anonymous. That was harder to swallow than a five-year-old gulping a spoonful of penicillin. Their answers were always quick, bordering on curt. They didn't wish to discuss the topic.

Naturally, I wondered why. They had the answer. Why were they lying, purposefully trying to dodge me? You didn't have to be Dick Tracey to realize that they were scared, even terrified of the topic. It was written all over their faces, and evident in their voices. *Two* questions kept me awake at night: What was the source of the fear? And what exactly had become of my find?

I fantasized about the momentous specimen finding a home in a lab. Maybe I could be a consultant. I did have a degree of expertise in the area of vertebrate paleontology. The piece of beautifully wrought paper I'd received at the end of spring semester would corroborate that. The semester came and went, barely giving my mind time to register that it was gone. I didn't have a chance to flood the market with job applications.,to take a breather, enjoy the summer weather, and hopefully hear back from a college, before the dreams began.

Maybe they weren't dreams at all. They weren't exactly visions of me digging up what I'd dubbed Aberrational Rex, but were similar. Sometimes I was a child, other times I was a teenager or young adult. There were instances when I was with family or friends, maybe even in my old backyard or in the school yard. The common denominator was that I and whoever accompanied me always extracted an enormous dinosaur fossil from the ground. The bone wasn't always a femur. Sometimes it was a vertebra or a gastralia (stomach rib cage) or a metatarsal, and it didn't always belong to a flesh eater. At times it was a species that was known, and others unknown.

They were *dreams* I told mysef, nothing more. Although I didn't know it at the time, these visions foreshadowed my future by interpreting my past. Then the nightmares began.

These new *things* weren't pleasant at all, but more vivid and potent, almost to the point where they stung my mind. I would wake up brushing cold sweat off my brow. They were certainly fantastical, but they were anything but fantasy.

It began as shapes. Basic, geometric shapes, forming and morphing like bubbles merging to the water's surface. There was color, but it was indistinct, bordering on stygian darkness. Still, the outlines of squares, rectangles, triangles and circles remained visible, like squeezing your eyes tightl after staring into the sun.

That's how they began, but they grew increasingly strange as time progressed. The shapes went from basic to amorphous blob-like shapes gyrating into sickening contortions.

Every night there seemed to be more and more additions, bizarre manifestations. Non-Euclidian. It was as if they had a fourth or even fifth and sixth dimension. Soon, voices accompanied them in tones both too high and too low to be categorized as human.

In the beginning, there was one voice whose vocal range covered both ends of the spectrum. Just like the shapes, there were more and more additions, to the point that all the sights and sounds became one jumbled mass of confusion. I initially mistook the voices for a foreign language, some ancient and outdated Sanskrit. The longer they continued, the more I realized the dialect was not native to any civilization we know.

These oniric messages were beyond unpleasant. And I noted one more correlation. The more I thought about Aberrational Rex. the more frequent the dream-like things rooted in my mind. I was never one to believe in coincidences. My parents taught me from a very early age that everything happens for a reason. God works in mysterious ways. Academia exposed me to other perspectives. Are war, famine, crime and disease part of God's plan? I was beginning to grow unsure of what to believe.

I had a feeling there were other beings or entities of higher, cosmic order with a different plan. If there was a big guy upstairs, would He let other deities pick on us lower lifeforms? Were others out there greater and more powerful than Him? In that case He wouldn't have much of a choice. But this wasn't the time to fall into a religious dilemma. There were bigger issues at hand, and I felt a growing certainty that religion had no dominion regarding my predicament.

Whether the nightmares were malignant, benign or ambivalent, I couldn't tell. These visions lasted roughly a month, a little less than four weeks. I remember the date they stopped. June 6th. The reason I can recall with such clarity is because they were replaced with something worse.

As I settled for the night on the sixth of June, I had the feeling that I was not alone. I was being watched. Now I know that sounds hokey, but it's the cold hard truth. I had company. It was like when you're in a room and your back is turned to the door. Somebody may walk in and you don't hear or see them, but you *feel* them. When I turned to look, there was nothing unusual, but I felt a rush. A powerful gust brushed past me, right *through* me.

It wasn't a physical force, like being bumped or pushed, more like being caught off balance in shifting wind. I felt lucky my ankle had not rolled under my foot. I had to extend my hands to prevent myself from falling. I noticed the blinds flapping as if whatever had whooshed past me tore through them as well. I adjusted them, hoping to see nothing outside but the shadows and silhouettes of suburbia at night.

A big, clunking vehicle was incongruously parked near the sidewalk. I got the impression of a very shiny black Cadillac. Nobody on my street drove such a car. Two men stood beside it. They seemed to be looking at me.

Darkness erased their facial features but they appeared to be wearing three-piece suits. I couldn't make out their arms and assumed they had them crossed or hands in their pant pockets. Our eyes locked. Breath fled my lungs. I turned away, then back.

only to find nothing there at all. The men and the care were gone.

The old here one minute gone the next trick, huh? Iit was almost laughable. I looked up and down the street in case they had somehow gotten into the care without opening or closing doors and sped away without starting the engine or squeeling their tires. Nothing. No car, no men in three-piece suits. *All in my head. Waking dream?* I closed the blinds and decided to let it go. Hopefully time would heal my condition.

ᚦ

Stephen cleared his throat. "This reminds me of what happened nearly a year ago," he said. "Gunner..." Mattie shriveled at the word. The others weren't listening. They appeared to be experincing the strange story in their own modes. Stephen went quiet. The story resumed.

ᚦ

The nocturnal visitations continued, but they were no longer relegated to the dark. A pounding on the door woke me one warm summer night. Tthrough the eyehole, I saw two men withf olive complexion in three-piece black suits cut several inches above their wrists and ankles. Both men wore dark shades.

I hesitantly opened the door and they simultaneously and robotically removed their sunglasses. Ttheir fingers were abnormally long, ther middle finger five to six inches from knuckle to tip. When they spoke, I was caught off guard. Their voices were comically high-pitched, and they spoke in a drawl and used slang terminology that had been outdated for quite some time.

I was shocked when the men mentioned the term Aberrational Rex, which I had never actually spoken aloud to a soul, nor wrote on paper, There was no way in hell they could have learned that moniker. Their warning was blunt. Drop it," they said, "never think about it again," and "absolutely never pursue it."

It wasn't so much the darkened tan of their flesh that compelled me to dread, but its hideously vascularity, strongly resembling some form of organic roadmap. The veins were blue and red. The blue veins sent bolts of ice– lighting through my spine, leaving a cold and desolate sense of mourning. The red veins radiated an invisible heat that burned me from within.

Their hideously bulbous eyes bore into my soul like ground-penetrating radar. They looked like fish eyes or frog. *Thyroid eyes*, I thought.

They replaced their sunglasses, turned and left. I watched them walk to their vehicle, feeling a sense of cool relief. It *was* a black Cadillac. This time I did see them get in, heard the ignition click, the engine turn over. Tailights strobed red as they drove away.

I closed the door rather sharply, locked it, then turned the dead-bolt for good measure. For several quiet seconds, I held a cellphone on my open palm and considered calling the police. Would they believe me? Would they laugh in my face like so many of my classmates had in middle school?

With a long sigh, I set my home security system on instant and tried to get some sleep. It was not to be. I rested my head on the cool and fluffy pillow only to experience one of the most broken nights of sleep in my life.

The porch incident wasn't the last I saw of those people. Were they government agents or officials, belonging to some secret and classified sect that perhaps the folks over at 1600 Pennsylvania Avenue didn't even know about? Maybe they were robots or cyborgs. They sure as hell walked, talked and moved like them. The thought of extraterrestrials did cross my mind, but then I got to thinking. *Why would they need to be from outer space?* They could have just as easily been inter-dimensional entities, beings hailing from some parallel or opposing plane of existence.

Whoever these people were, they were somehow familiar with me. Familiar enough to know that petty threats would fail to deter me and would only make me. I've always been a stubborn, pig-headed individual, and I'm proud to say that. Well, I *was* proud to say that.

♭

"The song's taking on new meaning for me," Eric said. "Right before the chorus here, he said something about entities living on parallel planes of existence. I'm guessing these black-suited weirdos may be lower-level guys, but I can't help feeling some connection to the cult that kidnapped Jay and I, even though those guys were more like druids in pajamas than government agents."

♭

A few weeks later I was eating breakfast downtown at Hazel's Restaurant and Coffee Shop when two men dressed like the other two walked in. Across the street, parked in front of a, bent and rusted parking meter, was an identical black Cadillac. It was slick despite its bulk, lack of color, and clunky-ness.

The two gentlemen were like the other two, only they were different too. One was comically tall and lank, the other short and round. They had the same olive complexion and the ungainly vascular skin and those uncomfortably long fingers.

Like clockwork, they removed their sunglasses and took their seats. Much to my surprise, their eyes didn't bug out of their skulls, but were instead narrow, slanted and squinty, and their facial features and bone structure was generally broader.

The waitress approached their table and filled cups with piping hot coffee. They watched this process with an absolute fixation that set me on edge. The waitress placed menus in front of them and told them she would give them a minute to decide.

The unwrapped their silverware and examined the utensils from top to bottom as if they'd never seen a fork, spoon or butter knife. I watched with equal fascination, or should I say *stunned* fascination as they switched silverware from hand to hand. The short one dropped a knife onto the table. The other shrugged subtly and dropped his knife too.

Their struggles resembled a *normal person* trying to steady a clunky, haphazard tool with their non-dominant hand. They couldn't manage it with either. A freakish sensation grew within me. I had to leave as quickly as possible. I wondered why these two came to Hazel's in the first place. Aside from making me aware of their presence, I could think of no reason.

I signtalled the waitress for my check. She seemed puzzled. I'd only sipped on a cup of coffee and hadn't eaten a bite of my omelette. I asked for a box to go. As she clicked her heels through the louvred doors into the kitchen, I kept a keen eye on the two strange men. It wast somewhat relieving to see they weren't paying any more mind to me than to other cutomers.

The theory of relativity kicked in. Though I couldn't possibly have waited more than a minute or two for the waitress, it felt like an hour. I paid cash, left several dollars for the tip, and made a beeline to the exit.

A shrill voice spoke as I opened the door. I was reminded of the voices that spoke in my nightmares. Hesitantly, I turned to find the two men had stood and were gazing expectantly.

"Excuse me?" I said. They did not react, no change in expression or evidence of recognition. I began to fidget. Perspiration beaded from my forehead. I

I tried again. "I'm sorry? Did you say something?" The two men glanced at each other.

The tall one stepped forward "What is it going to take?" he said in a shrill vibrato.

"I don't...I don't understand."

The short one spoke in a tinny tenor. "You comprehend. Now answer. What is it going to take?"

At a loss for even the most basic, monosyllabic answer, I glanced through the glass door at the Caddy across the street..

"You are making us take measures we prefer to avoid," the tall one said "You are going to wish you hadn't."

Is this for real? No one in the busy room was paying the slightest attention to us. *Walking nightmare?* I pushed the door open.

"Do not worry," the short one said. "We will be seeing you soon."

"Savor time you have," the tall one added. "Make it relative and make it last." They didn't laugh villainously or menacingly, and I didn't turn for a final look.

The door eased closed behind me. It took every molecule of my will not to make a run for it. When I reached my car, I didn't have to fumble for my keys. IThe door opened easily, I slid onto the bucket seat, and was on my way. Exactly where I was headed, I couldn't be sure. It's a miracle in retrospect that I didn't kill anybody driving in that trance-like state. I didn't want to deal with what had just happened or what had *been* happening. I couldn't face the sense of mortal dread that huddled behind my waking thoughts. I was in danger.

By the time I arrived home, I knew exactly what I had to do, what I should have done from the beginning of this horror. It would start with a phone call.

ᚦ

My uncle Dr. Edwin Gram was a professor of Anatomy and Physiology at the University of Pittsburgh, an expert in evolutionary theory specializing in foot morphology and mechanics. His research concerned bipedalism's progression from our knuckle-walking anthropoid ancestors to our hominid selves. He had guest-lecturerd at Kent State University about the discovery of *Ardipithecus Ramidus*, a 4.4-million-year-old human ancestor and had worked hand-in-hand with paleoanthropologists in the excavation of Lucy, a 3.2-million-year-old *Australopithecus Afarensis* from Ethiopia.

He also had a background in physics, but focused mainly on biomechanics aand the all-or-nothing theory of muscle fiber contractions. That theory states that only a certain percentage of muscle fibers contract when muscles are in use. Those that do contract, contract one hundred percent, the others not at all.

<p>

"I have to interrupt the movie for a second," Jay said. "This guy reminsds me of Stephen—at least career-wise—because Stephen... as long as I've known him, he's had an encyclopedic knowledge of physics, anthropology, and paleontology."

Jen nodded vehemently. "My old-time radio broadcast slash campfire story gives the same impression. I get the sense that this is real, or was real, and it parallels our reality. There's a weird vibe at work too. What the narrator describes must have happened in modern times, but a lot of the language sounds Victorian."

<p>

I hadn't spoken to Uncle Edwin in a while. I called the university and an operator transferred me to his office.

"This is Dr. Gram." His resonant voice sent ticklish vibrations through my ear. I remembered him discussing the big bang theory and Einstein's theory of relativity when I was young. He was well versed in Newton's laws and the notion of consciousness being transferred after death. *If an apple falls,* he once told me, *does the moon also fall?*

"Hey, uncle," I said."

There was a moment of silence. Maybe he didn't hear me, or maybe he was surprised to be hearing from me. The static cackling of a poor connection filled the void.

"Howard? What's new with my favorite nephew? Long time no interaction."

I told him about the dream-like visions that had stirred up this whirlwind of strangeness, the shapes and sounds, the geometric impossibilities, the dialects that human vocal cords couldn't possibly emit.

"Is this a prank?" he said levelly.'

"Of coures not," I said. "I woulnd't do that."

"Howard wouldn't, " Uncle Edwin said. "How can I know it's even youon the phone.?"

"Who else would it be?"

He chuckled. "There are 36,832 students on the main campus and another ten thousand or alumni who have attended my lectures over the years."

"It's me, I said. Howard. Howard Steven Gram."

"All right," he said. "If you are Howard, you can tell me what I gave you for your tenth birthday, right?"

"That's easy," I said with a grin. "*The Life of a Fossil Hunter* by Sternberg."

Another pause. "Okay, Howard. I'll take this seriously." Clearing his throat, as he always did before laying something heavy on me, he said: "People from all over the world have reported similar experiences. The experts, if you'd even want to call them that, probably more accurately the theorists, suggest that they aren't dreams or visions or hallucinations or even premonitions."

"Then what?"

"They classify is as out-of-body experience and claim people are spiritually whisked away to parallel or alternative dimensions to experience sights and sounds that would drive them insane if they were in their bodies." He sighed. "It's all a bit Lovecrafitan for my tastes."

ᛈ

"I hate to keep doing this," Amy said, "but this episode is familiar. Hasn't Stephen had similar out of body experiences with, you know, the *Mediums*...art, was it?"

ᛈ

"Is there more?" Undle Ewdin inquired.

I told him I had been receiving visits from the secret agents and described their olive complexions and vascular skin, their shrill voices, outdated slang and suits with cuffs way above their wrists and ankles.

"And those eyes," I said. "Their eyes—well some of their eyes–bug out like thyroid eyes. The others have slitted eyes, Oriental almost. They never blink."

"Men in black," Uncle Edwin said.

"I...I don't understand."

"This phenomena has been reported for ages. These 'Men in Black' usually drive black Cadillacs. Usually they are said to harass UFO witnesses and abductees. Most of the time they just threaten, tell peole never to speak of their encounters, stuff of that sort. In rare instances they're accused of attempting to pull witness into their cars."

"What can I do?" I said.

"Threats like you've described are very common, Howard. They usually tell people not to make them come back, or they don't want to have to come back or some variation of that. People tend to be so afraid that they listen, which is why paranormal researchers theorize a lot more people have encountered these

137

beings than come forward. Typically, Men in Black are attracted to paranormal hotspots, UFO sightings, strange lights in the sky, abductions, human sacrifice, farm animals being slaughtered and drained of their blood, Bigfoot and black panther sightings, that sort of thing."

This was too bizarre. My hometown was not a paranormal hotspot, not then and not before then. All the "paranormal" activity and madness seemed to be focused around myself. But there was something, maybe a reason for this.

The discovery of Aberrational Rex had been swept under the rug by government officials even better than Roswell and Area 51. I told Uncle Edwin of my discovery, a find which would rattle the bones of the dinosaur world down to its core, and its mysterious disappearance.

"Everyone involved refuses to speak of it. They want the science community to believe I made it up."

Uncle Edwin sighed. "This happens sometimes in the scientific community. It's usually swept clean, presumably by government agents. But there are a select few scientists like myself who do their due diligence and…"

"Wait," I interrupted. "You said this happens in the scientific community. Do you mean paleontology?"

"Primarily paleontology, but iother fields too, such as archeology and anthropology. Back when paleontology was still a relatively new, crude science, there were reports of field workers unearthing enormous bones that, if fully excavated, would prove to belong to be the tallest, longest and heaviest organism ever to have lived, even surpassing the blue whale."

He related how such bones had purportedly been found all over the globe. Some in the western United States, Montana, Texas, Colorado, Utah, Wyoming, North and South Dakota, some as far north as Canada. Others were from South America, Africa, China, Indonesia. No dinosaur in history represented such a wide range of evolutionary diversity and flourishing.

"Assuming it's true, of course," he added. "During the majority of the Age of Reptiles those landmasses were no longer the supercontinent known as Pangea, which existed during the late Paleozoic and early Mesozoic era. The largest dinosaurs didn't show up until the late Jurassic and early cretaceous periods. Anyway, no one has ever found the same bone more than once. They might discover a rib bone, metatarsal, vertebra or chevron bone, maybe even a tooth or claw, but never the same bone from a different animal."

"Wait," I said. "Are you suggesting there was only one of these animals? A single Aberrational Rex? How does that make sense? How would it reproduce?"

The phone started cutting out, interference of some sort. An indistinct voice, inhuman, robotic, alien, demonic, spoke a word or two of English. "Look." My uncle kept talking as if he hadn't heard a thing. "Up here," the voice said. "Wake up."

"Howard?" Uncle Edwin said. "Howard, are you there?"

An ear-splitting buzz erupted. I dropped the phone. A maddening hum invaded my skull. I pressed the heels of my palms tightly to my eyes. *Wake up*, echoed behind the noise.

Something hot seeped from my ear canal. When I wiped with the back of my hand, I was not surprised to see bright scarlet smears. Nausea assaulted my senses I stumbled for the sofa,and plopped onto the cool, soft leather. As I sank into the cushion, something caught my unwounded ear, an incessant beeping that would not end.

My ear throbbed. I smelled fish juice left to boil in a bucket on a muggy August afternoon. A heavy crashing sound resonated off the walls. I slowly craned my neck up to see two "Men in Black" silhouetted against the piercing white light that slipped through my open doorway.

They hooked their arms beneath mine and dragged me toward the cavernous maw where my front door had stood. A radiating white light beamed stabbing rays into my corneas. A metallic hum reverberaed my surviving eardrum. Before I could process another sensation I was engulfed by the energies beyond my door.

The light and I became one. Things darkened significantly, but it wasn't a darkness I can describe. Like the out-of-body experiences, this was something you could only experience spiritually, rather than physically. Even with your eyes shut as tightly as possible, your mind processes whatever fragments of light slip through. You can still process the blackness and picture the absence. I had no sense of sight at all.

I didn't wake in some variation of a high-tech laboratory. Nor was I strapped to an operating tablel. In fact, I found myself on my knees at the base of an immense alter. Next to me was Uncle Edwin. I'd thought it a shame to be *talking* to him under such unnatural circumstances, so you can imagine how I felt to *seei* him face-to-face within an even more unnatural predicament.

The altar was gold of the purest form. Whatever sound had emanated from the opposing plane to deprive me of my aural capabilities must have stunned my uncle as well. He was visibly disoriented.

The altar stood in the middle of a dark, cavernous hall that would have been at home in a wing of some ancient Gothic castle with towering architecture. I had a feeling there was no physical space beyond of our confine. Candles burned dimly, casting yellowish light. The sound of gongs reverberated. Space rippled. We had company.

Vaguely human forms entered single-file lines from dark, empty slots in physical reality. They wore flowing black robes with tall, pointed hoods. Only when they removed their hoods did I recognize the strange features of the "Men in Black." They weren't government agents, cyborgs or aliens, but an ancient cult. Why did I think of another cult from another place and time? Why did I think there was some connection? What did the term *Saint Joseph the Worker* mean?

ᛈ

"Jesus Christ," Jay said. "You'll never believe what this Howard guy says near the end of the movie."

"I heard it," Eric said. "This thing's playing out even longer than *Jesus of Suburbia*. There really is something to this."

ᛈ

"You are not in error," the man I assumed to be their leader informed us. "And since it is the truth you seek so fiercely that you would risk all mankind, it is the truth you shall receive." His eyes were of the narrow Oriental variety and his mouth was ovefilled with chiseled teeth. "What you call Aberrational Rex," he said, "we call Ram Diablo." I glanced at my uncle. He did not glance at me.

"Like so many scientists who unearthed the bones of Ram Diablo we so cleverly scattered about your globe, you have mistaken them for a clade of dinosaur. The truth is, Ram Diabl' does not belong to any clade."

"Then what does it belong to?" I said. Even this dire situation could not disuade my genuine interest.

"It is not *a* dinosaur at all but a primordial behemoth with traits of all dinosaurs and every kind of prehistoric life, even the most rudimentary organisms from the Pre-Cambrian era.

"Complex features of well-known giants, and the oddest details of pre-history's oddities such as Hallucigenia, Deinocherius and Platybelodon. Its chimeric attributes changed throughout the course of time, containing features of Miocene and Pleistocene megafauna. However, 'Ram Diablo' was wiped out sixty-five-million years ago during the great cretaceous-tertiary extinction."

I was baffled as was my uncle, but the cult leader explained in great clarity the idiosyncrasies of their fallen idol. Apparently, Ram Diablo was some vast cosmic entity possessing the physical and biological features of every prehistoric animal that had ever lived. These features were passed on to animals as they evolved, features such as thermoregulation, proto-feathers, four chambered hearts, camouflage, hollow bones and lungs filled with air sacks, compressed metatarsals, binocular vision, serrated teeth, biological weaponry such as septic bites, inertial feeding, flexible tail vertebra, acidic digestive juices and venom. There are far too many to list.

Prehistoric life evolved thanks to Ram Diablo, the "God" of the dinosaurs. Evolutionary advancements made by Ram Diablo were created through its own volition. It would adapt and then pass the necessary attributes to its spawn. Diablo had existed long before the creation of the earth, and possibly even the universe and settled in the stars of our universe just after the Big Bang."

Ram Diablo was a renegade, but also the most powerful and feared of its kind. After conquering others that dared to rebel against it, it ruled with an iron fist (or claw) over the stars in the universe, quick to obliterate whatever attempted to destroy or even disobey it. When the great creator gave birth to our world, Diablo saw an opportunity to take advantage.

The great creator intended to give life to man, who would eventually rise to become the dominant species on this planet. Ram Diablo attempted to prevent this by placing dinosaurs here. The prehistoric creatures I'd so loved and adored were not put here by God but an entirely different entity. Their purpose was to forever expunge us from the record books. Ram Diablo never intended to give us a chance.

This culminated with the great Cretaceous Tertiary Event. Cretaceous being the age of reptiles, tertiary being the age of mammals. An asteroid the size of Texas and weighing a trillion tons, sent by unknown powers, struck the gulf of the Yucatan peninsula. This effectively wiped Diablo's creations. Destroying its shared traits without giving the dinosauts a chance to ecologically diversify and evolve brought an end to the age-old cosmic nightmare.

Ram Diablo's bones were cast upon the earth. The only manner by which Ram Diablo could ever return would be if the skeleton were to be reassembled. The term "resurrect" was never used because that would imply Ram Diablo had died, which would be misleading. Such beings cannot truly perish. They are simply deprived of physical form and the matter which comprises its being reconfigured and made intangible—very much like pixels.

While the poisonously malevolent consciousness of Ram Diablo traversed hopelessly throughout the eternal abyss for sixty-five-million years, every bone of its anatomy was buried, hidden and scattered, smothered beneath millions of years of rock and dirt and sediment deposits, amidst impossibly tough terrain or, swept away and blanketed beneath the sands of time.

Ram Diablo's agents pointed a select few of us in the right direction and alas, there we were. These unrecognized agents were apparently higher on the pecking order than the Men in Black. All of them—members of this reptilian religion—answered to their version of our great creator. The great creator chose us because He sees His reflection in our image and wanted life to be as He intended it to be.

"Do you truly believe your Great Creator concerns himself with the likes of you?" these supposed friends and peers suggested. "If He did, why would He allow Ram Diablo to overlord His most prized creation for millions of years longer than our species has walked upright? If you think about it, he allowed God's creations, *our* God, the *real* God's creations, to survive into the modern day as the most graceful of creatures. Birds. He could have tried to stop this, but He didn't. He *couldn't*. He knows this planet, this life, doesn't belong to our kind. It belongs to the dinosaurs. We are but ants crawling in their kitchen."

Limited lighting surrounded the altar of the beast. I wasn't sure if running into the shadows would mean crashing into walls or floating off into a vortex of insanity. As a child I never fathomed that there are such nightmarish predicaments, let alone that I personally would encounter one. *How could you allow this?* I prayed. *If you're the loving, caring father everybody claims you are, how can you allow this to happen to your world?*

They didn't hold us against our will. There were no constraints nor did they attempt to surround us. With Ram Diablo loose again, we were damned. We got to our feet and ran. They didn't laugh or shout or call us fools or even try to stop us. We dashed into the darkness, and didn't find ourselves spinning or twirling or falling for all eternity. There was no stygian darkness, or vast and blank white madness. We were home.

ᚦ

"I've reached the boss level," Brian said. "This map is hellish. I have a feeling I'm about to be seeing this thing that wants to destroy this guy's world. Man, I hope it's not going to happen to us. It's ugly."

ᚦ

Something was wrong. *Everything* was wrong. The sky flamed with boiling blood and radiated doom. Screams rang out. Everything was in ruins. Houses crumbled, their structures flattened amid steaming mounds of brick and wood and glass. Smoking ruins that had once provided shelter for loving and comfortable family life lay everywhere. I dreaded to think of families unable to escape their dream abodes. Trees—massive, thick oaks and pines and maples—solid, dense and far from rotted, had been uprooted as if a child had plucked candles from an ice cream cake. The asphalt of the street cracked and crumbled. Cement sidewalks had been reduced to powde. Faint explosions and towering infernos marred the distance. I smelled the sizzling flesh.

Where my house once stood there was nothing more than a vacant patch of defiled land. I sensed whatever memories may have been created there were no longer viable. Ram Diablo had left nothing, not even an emotional imprint.

And that is when we saw the beast. To my horror, I was not repulsed, but mesmerized. Its sheer size was breathtaking, weighing more than 140,000 kilograms would require more buoyancy than our atmospher provides. Animal size is limited by basic geometry and the earth's atmosphere. And yet, here it stood. Its bones must be comprised of some impossibly strong substance. I know there are certain forms within the animal kingdom that cannot plausibly grow to gigantic proportions. For example, arthropods the size of cattle or horses that you see in horror and science fiction films cannot reasonably sustain such massive bulks; nor can non-human primates attain statures which would permit them to tear down buildings. Their anatomy would collapse like a neutron star. As far as I was aware, there was no anatomical form at all that could sustain such immensity.

Its general shape was that of a carnivorous biped nearly identical to therapods. A breathtakingly massive and dense skull was counterbalanced by an equally immense tail, which seemed surprisingly flexible despite thick, rope-like muscles flexing beneath seemingly impenetrable skin. Like the flesh–devouring dinosaurs it had conceived, Ram Diablo's head and tail leveled each other out, Earth's most nightmarish seesaw.

146

Its gaping maw revealed rows of teeth/fangs/tusks. I knew from my studies these would be quick to replace when lost. One row was blunt, the other blade-like, all serrated. Decaying flesh clung to the serrations. Its septic bite was probably the most lethal rendition of biological warfare ever. Aberrational Rex was very aberrational, Ram Diablo very diabolical. Although I could discern features of prehistoric life in it—Hook-like talons on its fingers and toes, flat, webbed claws and feet, a dank array of quill-like proto-feathers that blossomed into color-changing mammalian feathers along a chameleonic hide—I sensed this amalgamation was the antithesis of everything our lives stood for.

Its hind legs were stubby, rudimentary, only slightly longer than the vestigial forelimbs, allowing it to adopt a bipedal or quadrupedal gait. Horn-like buttresses hovered over its eyes. The eyelids themselves were membranous and multiple.

As I watched, National Guardsmen were being swept up in groups of thirty and forty and dissected by the beast's razor claws. Men and women turned to meat entered the the animal's cast-iron stomach to be digested by acidic juices and red-hot hunger. A tongue flicked from the apotheosis of all jaws, possibly tasting the air. At times, it wrapped that appendage around its adversaries and squeezed them dry. Noxious secretions and poisonous gases frothed from his nostrils.

No place in the wideworld was immune. Every tactic was exhausted. Tanks crunched like tin cans, missles merely annoyed the monster. Even nuclear weapons could not prevail, cauing more harm to evacuated cities than to their actual target. Radiation seemed only to feed its desire for destruction. Even when a wound was created, the creature's regenerative abilities quickly mitigated the harm. Damaged limbs healed or even replaced themselves at an unimaginable rate. \

These were merely some of the weapons this "God" employed to kill us off, not to mention the forces of nature it invoked. Earthquakes, tornadoes, tidal waves. Even its roar was deadly, engendering sonic booms that downed entire formations of jet fighters.

Now, I sit in an abandoned warehouse writing my journal and waiting for fate to claim me. I lost contact with my uncle in the course of our chaotic travels. Wherever he is, I hope he has found peace.

ᚦ

"I've reached the last piece," David said. "It's like a museum or art galler, collectibles as detailed as anything MacFarlane has produced. These are the most beautiful but horrible images and figures. I'm experiencing the same story you guys are listening to... or watching, playing, whatever. This monster is destructive and powerful, nigh invincible, but Stephen's enemy is smarter, a more powerful, perfected version."

ᚦ

Final Goodbye

It's dark and cold. There is no view to behold, nothing breathtaking, nothing inspiring. Not that any of that matters now. I've said everything I must. If anybody is out there, I hope that God (or whoever cares to help) will be with you. Before I go,

I offer my most sincere apologies for playing a part in this. I hope that whoever reads this will realize I am just a man comprised of flesh and bone. I cannot combat the sway that fate hods over me. I dare say it is *all* our fates. Extinction is inevitable, nothing more or less than natural. For whatever reason, I was chosen as a pawn to help bring about our downfall. This must be the closest that a human being has felt to being damned while alive.

We may have the entire world to hide in, but I'm finished running. I have a connection to Ram Diablo, as do those others who unearthed its bones through the ages, an intimacy that suggests wherever I go, it will follow, it will *find* me.

The earth trembles as I write this. I embrace what is coming. It's strangely ironic, really. Only two words matter now: Redemption, and… *Hope.* Farewell, friends. Whatever awaits on the other side, we will soon see.

6

W
ell, that was interesting," Jay said.

"Interesting?" Eric said. "I'd call it disturbing. I've read about mass-psychosis before."

"It was so sad," Amy said. "He died."

Jen shook her head. "We don't know that. Maybe he lived a long life."

"What does it mean?" David said.

"It means that what I've told you is real," Stephen said. "What happened here is going to be a picnic compared to what will happen to us if we don't do something."

"What are we supposed to do?" Jay said. "It's not like the story told us."

"I heard a premonition of death and damnation," Eric said. "It was damn near operatic."

"I know what we have to do," Stephen said. "I've been communicating with them for almost a year."

"You'll pardon me if we take that with a grain of salt," David said. "You've been acting crazy for a while, Stephen."

Everybody started talking at once. Stephen couldn't understand a word of it. He began to think that it was hopeless.

A voice cut through the clatter. "Listen to him." Mattie jumped to his feet. "He knows. I know too." He sagged back to his seat.

"We have to build an army," Stephen said. "We have to become an army. It's the only way to defeat Titan...the force behind this."

"I know," Eric said. "We have no experience or resources. It's not like we have military experience."

"Yeah," Jay added. "We're no soldiers."

Stephen sighed. He had them now. He met Mattie's eyes and grinned fiercely. "Here's the plan."

7

At midnight on Halloween, the group met at a pumpkin patch near Wampum, Pennsylvania. A single telephone pole stood amid the vines and rotted gourds. The telephone pole had a handmade sign tacked to it.

Dedicated to the memory of Ray
Robinson (1910-1985). "

He was The Green Man," Jay said. "When he was a kid, he was out here along this road flying his kite. It got tangled in electrical wires and the poor kid suffered third degree burns. When he got older, he only came out at night to hide his deformity. Moonlight gave his skin a greenish tint. Hence the legend."

"How terrible," Amy said.

"Is that why you brought us here?" David said.

"We need a place where veil is thin," Jay said. "And the witching hour on Halloween is ideal. Some people say they've seen the ghost of The Green Man in this area."

"I don't believe that stuff," Eric said, "but I see where you're going."

Mattie grabbed his head. "I feel it. It's like Gunner Bane magnified."

"Do you think you can draw him out?" Stephen said.

"I'll try." Mattie walked to the telephone pole and crouched. He put his hand on the pole and started mumbling. A keening sounded from everywhere at once.

Mattie shrank down even more and covered his ears, but kept mumbling. The pole started quivering,then shook violently. A greenish beam shot into the sky turning the underbelly of the clouds an olive color. The breeze became a gust, then a howling whirl twisted Stephen's hair.

"He was weak," Mattie shouted above the wind. "Your minion failed. He couldn't even defeat me."

The howl became a whine. Stephen had to lean into it to keep his balance.

"If he was created in your image," Mattie said, "he was weak. So, you must be weak."

Lightning sizzled. The pole splintered, throwing wood fragments across the field. The wooden shrapnel pattered around Stephen, a few striking his chest.

"Stand firm," Mattie shouted. "We must not fear." H stood straight and squared his shoulders. He looked as normal as he had in months. "I think it worked."

"Now what," Eric said.

"We have to trust the Mediums," Stephen said.

One by one, the Mediums took ethereal form. Literature looked studious and refined, wearing a Victorian waistcoat, top hot, and cane. He pulled a book from his coat vest beside his watch fob and began reading.

Cinema appeared as a young woman in a grey skirt suit with black trim. A tub of popcorn was tucked under one arm.

Art was a stocky man with an unkempt silver beard and wild eyes. He wore a dark tailcoat with brass buttons. He waved a palette before him.

Others appeared. Music, television, video games. These were even less defined. At the end of the line, a paleolithic man wore animal skins.

As Stephen watched silently, they formed a circle.

The wind died. They began chanting. A figure took form in the center of the circle. Stephen recognized it at once.

"Xyphactus."

"Isn't that one of your drawings?" David said.

The creature continued to take on substance until it stood twenty feet tall. Stephen admired the insectoid frame and finely detailed tattoos that covered its entire body.

"Beautiful," Mattie said.

Xyphactus stepped over Art and stood stolidly in the pumpkin field. Stephen felt a presence in his mind. All at once he was powerful. His thoughts were clear. He raised his arm and Xyphactus raised its arm. Stephen growled. Xyphactus growled.

Other creatures appeared and stepped into the field. Aeron resembled a miniature Boeing. Eric gazed wonderingly upon its metal hide. "I don't know what I'm feeling, but it's pretty damn cool."

David controlled Dimorphodon, a two-story saurian with bony plates protecting its vital areas. "You moved the neck frill," he said. "Great! I feel invincible." He turned in circles. The beast turned in circles too, massive tail trailing its long body.

Brian controlled Ghastonia. Jay controlled Styrax the humanoid triceratops. Amy, Jen and Ezzy controlled some of Stephen's newer creations. One was a tank, another had features of a Japanese Kaiju, and the last was a carnivorous, tropical plant.

"We have our army," David said.

"I feel like I could destroy the world," Jen said.

"I feel like I could protect it," Ezzy said. The plant wrapped leafy tendrils around Jen's creature.

"Let's hope it's enough," Stephen said. He looked toward the circle of Mediums. They were gone. "Can you bring him through, Mattie? Can you coax him that far?"

Mattie shrugged. "I can try." He tilted his face to the sky. "Not only are you weak, you're a coward."

The heavens rrumbled.

"Join the battle," Mattie shouted. "If you're not afraid."

A roar split the air. Clouds formed into jaws and slammed down. When they dissipated, Mattie was gone.

"It swallowed him," Ezzy said.

A voice sounded from the sky. "Come to me. If *you're* not afraid."

"What now?" Eric said. "Should I follow? I'm the only one that can fly."

"We don't have to fly," Stephen said. He focused his will on the place where he had met Titanos before. There was a vacuum pop and the pumpkin field became a vast, grey plain strewn with boulders. The sky was electric blue and yet still dark somehow.

The smell of burning flesh hung in the air and distant screams sounded continuously.

"What is this place?" David/Dimorphodon growled.

"This is the underworld," Jay/Styrax said. "Also known as Hades. A place that exists beyond the boundaries of known, scientific reality."

"Says the dinosaur," Jen said through her Godzilla-like avatar.

The ground shook. A shadowy figure moved towards them. *Titanos*, Stephen thought, and he didn't feel afraid thinking it.

"It must be huge," Brian/Ghastonia said.

"It only appears huge," Stephen said. "It's small inside."

Titanos continued toward them. Each footstep vibrated the bedrock. And still it came. Stephen began doubting himself.

By the time it stopped, it towered over even Aeron. Anatomically, it resembled a man with a massive, tyrannosaurus-like build. Its head was of a carnosaur variety with protruding fangs. Its body was striped in what looked like Native American warpaint, and it carried a weapon the size of the telephone pole it had shattered. One end was an axe made of black metal glazed in blood.

Mattie? Stephen thought.

"That thing must be a hundred feet tall," David said. His neck frill expanded. "How are we supposed to beat that?"

"Together," Stephen said.

8

Stephen shot towards Titanos. He raised his arm and Xyphactus's sword raised too. *It's as if I am him.* The weapon crashed into Titanos's armor. Sparks flew. *No, the unarmored side.* While the avatar was largely under his control, it had volition of its own.

Titanos' arm swept down and threw Xyphactus across the cavern. Stephen's avatar impacted a boulder with a sickening crunch. Pain ripped through him. *This isn't going to be easy.*

Dimorphodon pounded toward Titanos with Ghastonia closely behind. Twin blades flashed in the meager light. Dimoprhodon slammed into Titanos' leg. His neck frill crunched.

Titanos' leg buckled. He went to one knee. Ghastonia's blades slashed faster than the eye could follow. Tendrils of black ichor flew from the wounds they inflicted.

Titanos' barley noticed. With a rock shattering roar, it grabbed Ghastonina with one hand. Its claws wrapped around his entire torso and pinned his arms to his side. Ghastonia cried out. The sound of crushing bones echoed.

Stephen struggled to his feet. Jolts of pain shot through his ribs. He couldn't breathe. Where Titanos' ichor had fallen, steam rose from the stone floor. *How can we possibly defeat this monster?*

"Together," he muttered. He had to believe in something. They couldn't let Titanos destroy humanity.

Mist spewed from Dimorphodon's snout directly into Titanos' face and eyes. The gargantuan creature flinched. Its eyes slapped closed. It flung Ghastonia away. Brian-Ghastonia landed in a crumpled heap.

Dimorphodon drove his neck frill into Titanos' thigh. Bony plate sank into flesh. Titanos ripped Dimorphodon away. A wet slurp sounded. The wound sealed.

With a grunt, Titanos cast Dimorphodon aside. Stephen braced as the dinosaur tumbled toward him. *That's my brother,* he thought.

He extended his arms and tried to brace himself against the impact without hurting David. Xyphactus's sword arm contacted first. Stephen watched in horror as the blade sank deep into Dimorphodon's flesh.

"I'm sorry" Stephen said. "I forgot" Guilt poisoned him. "You bastard!" He charged.

Styrax' armored girth was pinned beneath Titanos' massive foot. He was the largest of them, but looked like no more than a road bump.

The T-Rex flopped back and forth as Titanos moved, her teeth embedded in its leg. The tank fired round after round.

Each one impacted with a squishy thump.

Titanos' fist slammed into the T-Rex's head. She lay motionless, head contorted at a wrong angle.

Titanos turned to Stephen. A dozen or more teeth were still embedded in its leg.

With a screeching roar, Stephen launched into battle. His arms became a blur of metal. The ground rumbled. Vines erupted from crevices in the bedrock. They stretched upward sinuously, hundreds of them. Fronds opened, revealing a lighter green color and parrot-like beaks.

Stephen's foot caught. He skidded headlong.

Spores sprayed from the plant's beaks, drenching Titanos in a gooey mist. The monster growled and flailed as vines entwined its arms and legs. Stephen crawled to his feet. The battle was turning.

With a jerk of the wrist, Titanos severed one vine and then another. Its head lunged forward. Its jaws clamped shut on a frond-head. Sap spurted. A keening wail sounded. The plant released its grip. Parrot beaks opened and froze in mid shriek.

Ezzy! Stephen's right arm slashed even as his left arm descended. The sword blade struck Titanos. It was like hitting concrete. Still the blade bit. Black ichor oozed.

The edge of his shield-arm struck Titanos' wrist. The clawed hand severed and dropped to the floor. Titanos' roared. Its remaining hand swung around. Stephen went spinning. He didn't even feel the pain until he stopped.

Tank-Amy-advanced. The shells seemed better aimed now striking Titanos' face repeatedly. Shrapnel and scales exploded into the dark. Titanos raised its arms defensively, clawed hands spread.

Hands. Not one but two. The stump had already regenerated. Stephen wanted to yell retreat. It was already too late. Titanos foot stomped down, crushing the turret.

"Amy," Stephen screamed. He tried to stand but couldn't. His leg twisted.

"Why do you persist?" Titanos said. "Obviously you have no chance. You never had a chance. This world is my whim. I can devour it whenever I wish."

"Then why don't you?" Stephen said.

"Because I didn't wish it…until now. All I have to do is close my eyes and unthink you."

Its eyes closed. Stephen cringed. *At least we tried.*

Nothing happened. Titanos' eyes reopened. "You're still here."

"Of course, they are." Mattie's face appeared. It was as large as Titanos' and hovered at its eye-level. "Do you think you're the only one who can imagine?"

Vaporous forms emerged from the broken avatars. Stephen recognized them: Literature, Cinema, Music, Oral Storytelling, Video. They combined into a humanoid body, supporting Mattie's head. Stephen could see through the body, but it seemed real anyway.

"We belong here," Mattie said. "You do not. We are in harmony with the human mind. You are a contradiction, spawned of a Greek Titan and Cthulhu."

"No! How…?" The dragon-like face shifted. Stephen sensed confusion, maybe fear.

Titanos unstrapped the deadly hybrid weapon from its back. The axe end glinted despite the darkness. The sword end was hidden in shadow.

"Die!" The sword slashed through Mattie'schimeric body without effect. The axe sliced through his face.

Mattie smiled. "You have no power here. Not now. We know what you are." He reached into Titanos' chest and squeezed. When the hand returned, it held a black, crystalline mass.

Spittle spraying from Titanos' mouth. "How is this possible? This cannot be."

"No, *you* cannot be," Mattie said.

A fissure erupted at the crown of Titanos' head and spread downward through his snout, chest, and abdomen. The halves of its body fell.

Smaller fissures appeared. Pieces of the body broke off, smaller and smaller until they were the size of ants that scurried off in every direction. A few crawled over Stephen's damaged foot. He brought his good foot down on top of a swarm. It made a satisfying crunch.

9

That was wild," Brian said. "That dude was badder than Clayface in *Batman Arkham Asylum*."

"Yeah, it was," Jay said. "But it was real."

"Was it?" Eric said. "It seems more like a case of collective hallucination."

"That was no hallucination," Jen said. "My neck's still throbbing where the bastard pounded me."

"Your avatar," Brian said.

"Kiss my avatar, Brian," Jen said. "I felt it, that was me."

The scene played out in Stephen's mind. He felt a mix of relief and anxiety. The battle was over. They had apparently won. But at what cost? He visualized David's avatar motionless on the stone floor, blood pooling around it. *My brother's dead.*

"David's gone," Ezzy said in a low voice. Her arms were covered in red welts. Her face too. A tear dripped from one eye. Stephen wanted to hug her, but couldn't make himself move. It wasn't just that his muscles ached, but the connection between his mind and body had frayed.

"And Mattie," she said with a gulp. "He saved us you know?"

"Here's to Mattie," Eric said. He lifted a tumbler half-filled with golden liquid.

"You're paying me for that," Stephen said. "That's my D-Day Dewar's." He bit down. *What could be more D-Day than this?* He grabbed an empty glass from the end table and lifted it. "And here's to David."

Glasses and cans clinked throughout the room. "Fallen warriors," Jay said. "Every important victory exacts a price."

"I wish there was some way to go back in and see them," Ezzy said. "I never told David how much I loved him."

"He was a better brother than I was," Stephen said.

"Life is never truly gone," a familiar voice echoed. *Art*, Stephen thought. It was the first Medium he'd encountered.

A panel hovered in midair like a museum piece. Mattie sat on an examination table. His hair was cut short, his nails were kempt. He looked like a regular human being.

"Terminal," a doctor in green scrubs said.

The image wavered. A new scene appeared. Mattie, in a dark living room. An obese man sat on the couch. Gunner Bane loomed from the shadows. Stephen's gut clenched. He never hated anyone as much as Gunner Bane...until he experienced Titanos.

Gunner Bane touched the man and his body burst into dust.

"Jesus," Amy said. "Is this what Mattie went through? No wonder he was damaged. That must have been his father."

The next image was tinted amber. They saw shapes and movement but no details.

Brian crumpled his hard cider can. "What the—"

The image shattered, revealing a giant version of Stephen.

An image flashed of Mattie and Stephen creeping down steps at the church where the cult had held Eric and Jay captive.

The next image showed a blade severing Gunner Bane's head from his body. The head flew into Titanos' gaping jaws. *Crunch*.

Stephen's living room appeared with the group arranged pretty much as they were now. Only David was there and Mattie was there. The rest of them didn't look like they'd been beaten.

Now they were in a dark place, approaching in their avatar forms. Stephen's throat clenched as David charged. It looked so powerful and determined with his scythe-like fan and pounding legs.

Chaos. Images flashed faster than Stephen could keep track. Bodies flew, blood spewed. He glimpsed Ezzy's vines rising from the floor, and then it was over.

The display went dark. A single bio-card hung in midair. A spotlight shone on its face. Dinobot. His mouth moved. "Life reconfigures itself."

The spotlight shifted to the empty spot on the sofa. Mattie appeared. His form was misty and flickering.

"It's okay, guys," he said. "We did it."

"How did you do that?" Stephen said. "How did you destroy Titanos?"

"Yeah, man, that was amazing," Brian said.

"It destroyed itself," Mattie said. "Its nature. Its power may have been formidable, but it came from a contradiction. Its essence was formed from two antithetical forces. When I forced it to understand its nature, the binding broke."

Mattie's form stood. "I have to leave now. The Mediums are not omnipotent."

He turned and walked into the mist toward the obese man and a woman who must be his mother. There was also a dog.

The images collapsed. Someone touched Stephen's shoulder. He turned to find David. His skin was luminescent.

"David!" Stephen threw his arms around his brother. They passed right through David's form.

"Don't worry, big brother," David said. "We'll meet again." The Mediums huddled around them. Art, cinema, literature, music, video. Their warmth was like a fire to Stephen's chill. They turned as one and led David into the light.

Afterword

I've never worked as hard on a book as I have on *Mediums*. The original draft was handwritten—I wanted to do it that way because I was also doing the illustrations, so I truly felt like an artist—and it came out to 654 pages. Typing all of it was laborious, although I made some serious revisions while doing so. After the third or fourth draft, I think we managed to turn a lump of coal into a nice, trim diamond, hence the novella you hold in your hands. Sorry about the bad metaphor. In any case, this was a labor of love, and I really hope that it shows in the final product. When I set out to complete the trilogy I'd envisioned a number of years ago, I knew I wanted the third chapter to be about all of the things that interest me and that I love: all the different artforms that exist in cultures.

Speaking of the trilogy, it began with *Perspectives*, my metafiction novel, which was followed by *Haunted Farm* (originally published as *Haunted Revengeance*) and ends with this work. Tonally, *Perspectives* and *Haunted Farm* are much more in alignment than *Mediums*, so in that sense, it can be considered a spiritual, or loose, sequel, one that can be enjoyed just as easily in standalone form as it could the final bookend of one huge story. If you've read the first two books, you will enjoy some of the references/connections, such as Stephen and David running across a copy of *Perspectives* in the YSU bookstore, and the killer from *Haunted Farm's* cameo appearance.

I ultimately had two goals in mind when I wrote this book. The first was to write about how our imaginations can act as bridges between seemingly disparate concepts such as religion and science, hence the connection between Greek Mythology and Lovecraft's mythos. The second was to create my own ultimate villain, a supreme baddie that embodied power and terror unlike anything comprehensible. Enter Titanos. I had drawn the image on the front cover many times over the years, so I knew what he would look like. Coming up with his story was even more fun. I hope you enjoy my illustrations as much as the story. In the end, art has the ability to uplift every one of us.